THE "WONDERFUL" WIZARD OF FUTHERMUCKING OZ

THE "WONDERFUL" WIZARD

OF FUTHER-MUCKING OZ

MATT YOUNGMARK
AND THAT BASTARD, L. FRANK BAUM

atherton
HAIGHT

ATHERTON HAIGHT, SEATTLE

First edition, March 2017

atherton
HAIGHT

The Atherton Haight logo is registered trademark of Atherton Haight.

WWW.YOUNGMARK.COM

Cover illustration by Mona Finden
Copyright page and back cover illustrations by W.W. Denslow

Library of Congress Cataloging-In-Publication Data
is available on request.

ISBN 13: 978-0-9840678-7-9
ISBN 10: 0-9840678-7-6

FOR
DAWN MARIE PARES.

———————

Once again, forever, always.
I wouldn't even be someone who could
write this book without you.

TABLE OF

CONTENTS.

EDITOR'S NOTE.

Arabella Grimsbro curses like a longshoreman. After careful consideration, we have decided that altering her language, as profane as it may be, would irreparably damage both the tone of her prose, and, in some cases, its very meaning.

If you are considering purchasing this book for a child, please be aware that, among other obscenities, it features some variant of the word "fuck" eighty-seven times.

(Eighty-eight if you include the editor's note.)

INTRODUCTION.

n L. Frank Baum's intro to *The Wonderful Wizard of Oz*, he claimed his goal was to write a fairy tale without the violence and endless moralizing of Hans Christian Andersen and the Brothers Grimm (he also, for the record, called children "youngsters," and stated that his goal was "to pleasure" them, but whatever).

If that's true, I'd say he sucked at his job, because that book contains some *fucked up shit.*

I often wonder what my life would have been like if I'd had the good sense to stay the hell away from a place called Voyages Through Literature, or skipped the godforsaken mall altogether, and told Madeline she could deal with her stupid crush on her own. In the end, though, I suppose you could say the decision was mine. I personally selected *The Wonderful Wizard of Oz* from a list of truly awful-sounding public domain classics, clicked "yes" to agree to whatever the terms and conditions were, and stepped into that tacky neon booth of my own free will. But, in my defense, *they offered me money.* It was clearly entrapment, and you bet your sweet ass that if I can ever prove that the store actually exists—if it isn't some portal to an alternate dimension or my own brain finally severing all ties to reality—I fully intend to sue.

My name is Arabella Grimsbro, and this is the worst thing that's ever happened to me.

CHAPTER 1

THE CYCLONE.

irst off, I'd like to make it clear that I've never even been to Kansas. When you find yourself in a situation as batshit crazy as I did, you kind of roll with it, which I guess is why I brought Kansas up to begin with. For me, every time I said "Kansas," or someone repeated it back to me, it just kind of meant "reality in general." Or, specifically, Calabasas, California, where I lived in a perfectly normal apartment with my Mom.

My Mom is the coolest, smartest, and honest-to-God most beautiful human being I've ever known. She was born in Peru, looks like a straight-up runway model, and will absolutely punch you in the face if you piss her off. She's usually working some kind of boring office job, but what she really is, deep down in her soul, is an *entrepreneur*. She just hasn't quite gotten any of her business ideas up and running yet. I inherited some of her smarts, all of her ADD, and, despite what she'll tell you, exactly none of her good looks. In terms of hotness (or lack thereof) I take after my Dad, who is your standard-issue generic pan-European white guy mutt. The truth is, I don't really know that much about him.

And before you start speculating that my Dad is a Secret Fairy Prince from a Faraway Magical Land, he's not. He's just some schmo. He used to sell cars, and now he sells syndicated television shows to local affiliate stations. Which I guess is a decent living, because to whatever extent broadcast TV still exists, they still need to fill interminable hours with reruns of *The Ghost Whisperer* or whatever. He lives, like, barely half an hour away in Studio City, but I never see him.

Anyway, this book isn't about them. It's about lions and scarecrows and that fucking asshole wizard, and it begins, of all places, at the mall.

The reason I even went to the stupid mall that day was because Madeline needed moral support. There are exactly three lesbians in our entire high school, and my friend Madeline and her hopeless crush, Amber Maldonado, are two of them. When Amber Maldonado snaps, Madeline comes running. It's not that their whole deal threatens our friendship or anything like that—I have my crushes, too. It's just that I acknowledge that Peter Zamora is a sneering, petulant twit who just happens to look *amazing* in a black peacoat. Madeline, on the other hand, keeps insisting that Amber Maldonado actually has a single redeeming quality.

Amber asked Madeline to join her at the mall with her equally-horrible group of friends, and Madeline asked me to come along, because the prospect thrilled and terrified her in equal measure. Only she didn't want me *with her* with her—as I said, Amber and her crowd are the literal spawn of Satan, and I'm happy to say that to their faces—so we agreed to meet at the vibrating massage chairs by the food court when she texted me in tears that the whole thing had fallen apart in whatever spectacular way it inevitably would.

So there I was, limbs splayed across a currently-motionless vibrating chair, scrolling through what I didn't even know were probably the LAST TUMBLR POSTS I WOULD EVER SEE, when I noticed the sign. I'm about 90 percent sure the place used to be a Build-A-Bear Workshop, but it apparently went out of business (possibly because why, in all of recorded history, would anybody want to *build a bear*). Now it was something called Voyages Through Literature, which looked like the type of wholesome, educational crap that would be boarded up and replaced with a Hot Dog on a Stick inside of three months.

Oh my god—junk food. It's been *so long*. I could tear through a hot dog on a stick like a school of piranha skeletonizing a cow right now. You don't even *know*.

The place didn't even seem to have any actual books in it, just various screens displaying videos… *about* books? I'm certain that I would have never set foot inside it, except some beleaguered dad plopped his screaming toddler down on the chair next to me in an attempt to reattach a shoe or something, and my peaceful, non-vibrating solitude was shattered. At least the abandoned video book store looked quiet.

Alas, the woman behind the counter pounced on me the moment I entered. She was maybe forty-ish, with 1950s cat-eye glasses, curves bursting out all over the place, and a red dye job in some kind of weirdly complicated up-do. Her smile was wide, but felt pretty mandatory. "Welcome to Voyages Through Literature!" she said with more than a hint of desperation. "Where can we transport you to today? 19th century England? The frozen wilds of the Canadian wilderness? A pirate frigate adventuring on the high seas?"

"How about the 74th annual Hunger Games," I said noncommittally, tapping on one of the touch screen kiosks. "I could do some fucking *damage* with a composite bow."

"Um, I don't think we have that one," she said. "But if it's action you're looking for, perhaps Alexandre Dumas's timeless classic, *The Three Musketeers*?"

Swiping through the selections, it quickly became clear that the shop didn't carry a single book that had been published within the past eighty years. *Robinson Crusoe*? *Ivanhoe*? Whatever the hell a *Scarlet Pimpernel* was? A better name for the place would have been Voyages Through Public Domain Books That Are So Old Nobody Owns the Copyright Anymore So We Don't Have to Pay a Licensing Fee.

"You know what? I'm good."

"Are you sure?" the woman said. "It's a *total immersion* experience. You'll swear that you were actually there!"

Actually *where*? Some sweaty old playwright's creepy imagination?

"Yeah, I'm supposed to meet my friend…"

"Listen, we're still in the market research phase," she said. And this is the part where I should have realized that she was *way* too desperate. "If you're willing to fill out a brief survey about your voyage, we can offer you $20 for your trouble."

I looked at my phone—Madeline hadn't texted. For all I knew, it could be hours before she did. And you know, twenty bucks is twenty bucks. At the very least, filling out the form would probably be good for a few laughs. What the hell, I figured.

What the hell.

I continued browsing through their selection—there was a lot of stuff I'd never heard of, and most of what I had didn't sound particularly appealing. The thought of being totally immersed in a Charles Dickens novel sounded like actual punishment, and ugh, *definitely* nothing by Jane Austen. I almost settled on something called *A Princess of Mars*, because that sounded like a pretty messed-up fairy tale. But then I saw it. *The Wonderful Wizard of Oz*, by L. Frank Baum. I had seen the movie a bunch of times—my Mom and I used to watch it together about once a year, like a special occasion. When I was *really* little it genuinely scared me, and even as I got older, the over-the-top campiness and weird sincerity of the whole thing still held a secret, special place in my heart.

So I figured I could kill some time on the Yellow Brick Road. At the very least, I'd know the songs. I made my selection on the screen, then scrolled down through eight or ten pages of miniscule text and clicked "accept" on the terms and conditions (I can't even *imagine* what was actually in there).

"So, is there a headset or something?" I asked the sales lady. "Is this like an Oculus Rift kind of thing?"

"Just step inside the booth, sweetie," she said. "We'll take care of every-thing." Her expression had changed subtly, with eyes slightly wider, smile just a tad more forced. I suppose this should have been another warning sign, but whatever. Old people are weird. The booth itself was built into the back wall of the shop, and plastered with brightly-lit exclamations. WONDER! ADVENTURE! I swear to god, one of them said EDUTAINMENT! It looked exactly like the kind of door you'd build if you were trying to lure children inside to harvest their organs (in retrospect, *I wish*).

Inside, it was so dark I couldn't even tell how big it was. I reached out my hands for the back wall, but found nothing. "Safe travels," the sales lady said softly as she closed the door behind me.

And, just like that, I was engulfed in darkness.

We didn't have *cyclones* in Southern California, but we did have earthquakes, so when the floor suddenly lurched beneath my feet, that's what I assumed was happening. *Oh my god*, I thought, *this is how I'm going to die. Trapped under a collapsed ceiling in the back room of a mall shop that I'd be embarrassed to be found dead in, before they can even harvest my organs.* Then the room was spinning, and I lost my balance. Somewhere, a little yappy dog barked.

To this day, I maintain that I did not faint. I hit my fucking head or something.

Either way, though, I was out like a light.

THE COUNCIL WITH
THE MUNCHKINS.

I was awakened with a shock, so sudden and severe that if I had not been
lying on a soft bed (somehow?) I probably would have banged my head
and knocked out a goddamn tooth or something. First off, there was a
gross, wet dog nose in my face, whimpering.

Holy shit. "Toto?"

Sure enough, the dog leapt off the bed, hopped up and down on the
dirty wooden floorboards, and barked. It was a small black terrier, and
looked *exactly* like the dog from the movie. I started to remember where I
was—or, at least, where I was *supposed to be*—but having an actual dog in
the room with me seemed over the top. I mean, *whose dog was it*? Did the
sales lady take it with her to work every day, just in case somebody chose
The Wizard of Oz? What kind of livestock did she have back there for the
sorry sons of bitches who picked *The Jungle Book*?

I clawed at my face briefly, but there was no virtual reality headset or anything. Apparently, the dog really was there. The inside of the

EDUTAINMENT! booth turned out to be a dingy room done up like a wooden farmhouse with two beds (*bow-chicka-wow-wow*), a rusty wooden stove, and not much else. At least it was bright now, with what looked like sunlight flooding the room though a small window. I walked slowly over to it, with Toto yipping at my heels the entire way.

The window showed a surprisingly realistic, overwhelmingly colorful nature scene, complete with green hills, lush trees swaying in the breeze, a babbling brook—the whole deal. So, a video screen to watch the story through, built into a generic, dingy room that could be in just about any book written a million years ago. The setup was actually somewhat charming in its way, I had to admit, but it was hardly "total immersion." That was the second criticism I'd put down on my $20 market research form, I decided, right after KNOCKING ME OUT AND ALMOST KILLING ME.

I'm not even sure what I thought when I opened the door expecting the interior of the mall, only to discover more majestic wildlife. Before I could even marvel at the scope of it all—seriously, it was a 360 degree, panoramic view, I didn't even know they made video screens that big—I noticed a group of weird little people approaching.

And by little people, I mean like human beings with dwarfism. They were roughly as tall as your average ten-year-old, three men dressed all in blue from their pointy hats to their polished boots, and a little old lady in a sparkly, pleated dress. The men stopped short and looked a bit scared of me, but the woman marched right up close.

"You are welcome, most noble Sorceress, to the land of the Munchkins," she said in a sickly-sweet old lady voice. "We are so grateful to you for having killed the Wicked Witch of the East, and for setting our people free from bondage."

"Oh, shit," I said. "We're actually doing this. Are you people *actors*? Do they hire *actors* for this?"

It didn't make any sense. A dog was one thing, but how many public domain books could possibly have *little people* in them, that they would have *four little people actors just hanging around on call?*

Or did they *specifically knock me out so they could call the casting agency and set all this up*? Jesus, how long had I been unconscious?

The old woman basically ignored me and continued her speech. "Or your house did, anyway," she said, "and that is the same thing." She pointed to the corner of the house behind me. "See! There are her two feet, still sticking out from under a block of wood."

I turned to look, and actually screamed. Just as she had said, two feet were sticking out from beneath the house. The shoes on them were silver rather than sparkly red like the ones I remembered from the movie. But what really shocked me was *all the blood*. Blood was everywhere. And, like, *sinews and stuff*. Pretty much what you'd expect to see, I guess, if an *actual person* had been crushed to death by a falling domicile.

"What kind of fucked up *Wizard of Oz* snuff flick is this? Do you let *children* come in here?"

"She was the Wicked Witch of the East," the old woman said calmly. "She has held all the Munchkins in bondage for many years, making them slave for her night and day. Now they are all set free, and are grateful to you for the favor."

"Right," I said, regaining a bit of my composure. "Of course. You're a Munchkin."

"No, but I am their friend, although I live in the land of the North," she said. "When they saw the Witch of the East was dead, the Munchkins sent a swift messenger to me, and I came at once. I am the Witch of the North."

Hmm. Maybe the casting agency was short on 1930s glamor-types, but had plenty of extra little folks. At least it subverted the whole good-witches-are-beautiful, evil-witches-are-hideous-crones trope. This woman was *not* cute.

"Look, I get that you went to a lot of trouble for this," I said. "And hopefully you'll still get paid. But seriously, get that sales lady back in here. I'm done."

"Who is the sales lady?" inquired the old woman.

"Enough! The sales lady! At the crappy video book store, in the mall!" I made a complete circuit, walking all the way around the crashed farmhouse, and didn't see an exit door anywhere. How big *was* this place? Could it all be behind the storefront? Holy shit, had they *transported me to a second location*?

The Witch of the North seemed to think for a time, with her head bowed and her eyes on the ground. Then she looked up and said, "I do not know where The Mall is, for I have never heard that country mentioned before. But tell me, is it a civilized country?"

"Jesus Christ."

"In the civilized countries, I believe there are no witches left, nor wizards, nor sorceresses, nor magicians," she continued. "But, you see, the Land of Oz has never been civilized, for we are cut off from all the rest of the world. Therefore we still have witches and wizards amongst us."

"You're going to make me go see the motherfucking wizard, aren't you."

"You know of Oz, the Great Wizard!" the Witch said. Then she sank her voice to a whisper, like she was scared even to mention him in conversation. "He is more powerful than all the rest of us together! He lives in the City of Emeralds."

I was about to register another complaint, but suddenly one of the Munchkins gave a loud shout. The three of them had been standing there so quietly the whole time that I had assumed they were being paid as extras and weren't allowed to talk.

"What is it?" the old lady asked. Then she looked at the house and started laughing. The feet of the dead witch had disappeared entirely (along with, thankfully, all the blood and gore). Nothing was left but the silver shoes.

"She was so old," explained the Witch of the North, "that she dried up quickly in the sun. That is the end of her. But the silver shoes are yours, and you shall have them to wear." She reached down and picked up the shoes, and after shaking some dust out of them (a nice touch), handed them to me.

"The Witch of the East was proud of those silver shoes," said one of the blue guys. It turned out he had a speaking part after all. Maybe SAG rules were different for back room mall theater productions. "And there is some charm connected with them, but what it is we never knew."

The slippers! Of course! Now I knew how to put an end to this charade.

I kicked off my shoes and put them on. They fit surprisingly well, but then again, considering how elaborate this whole thing was, it wouldn't have been that much extra trouble to measure my sneakers while I was unconscious. As soon as they were on, I stood up straight and clicked my heels together three times.

When I opened my mouth to speak, however, no sound would come out.

What the fuck? I knew the words well enough. *Everybody* knew the words. I tried again, and my lips moved just as expected, but once again, silence.

I stopped for a moment to think. All of this was clearly from the *Wizard of Oz* book, rather than the movie. There was no bustling Munchkin township, or creepy candy union representatives, or elaborate dance number. You'd think the movie would be the one to skimp on all this stuff, since a novel didn't have to pay actors and costume departments and all that, but whatever. The thing was, the book was at least a century old, but the movie hadn't come out until 1939. The movie stuff wasn't in the public domain yet.

Was it possible that I wasn't allowed to mention anything that was still under copyright by MGM? How could they *physically prevent me* from doing so? This was my first hint that I had gotten myself involved with something much, *much* worse than a goofy-ass hybrid of virtual reality and community theater.

It made the notion of a quick exit all that much more appealing. Perhaps I could paraphrase? "There's no... *location*... that approximates... the *place where you live*?" I clicked my heels again.

Nothing. Of course, if the classic line wasn't from the original text, there must be some other password altogether. Hmm. What would the moral of a hundred- year-old children's book be? "There's no place like eugenics and racism?"

Historical figures from the previous century were *always* into eugenics and racism. If I knew as much about L. Frank Baum then as I do now, I might have said, "There's no place like LITERALLY ADVOCATING GENOCIDE" (it's a real thing, look it up!). Regardless, however, I did not manage to end the simulation, or whatever the hell was going on there. The Munchkins and the old lady just looked at me like I was crazy.

"Fine," I said miserably. "How do I get home?"

The Munchkins and the Witch first looked at one another, and then at me, and then shook their heads.

"At the east, not far from here," said one of the Munchkins who hadn't spoken yet, "there is a great desert, and none could live to cross it."

"It is the same at the south," said the other one. At least they were all getting a line in, which hopefully meant they would be making more than TWENTY FUCKING DOLLARS for suffering through this indignity. "I have been there and seen it. The south is the country of the Quadlings."

"Sure. Quadlings," I said.

"I am told," the original Munchkin who had yelled about the Witch said, "that it is the same at the west. And that country, where the Winkies live, is ruled by the Wicked Witch of the West, who would make you her slave if you passed her way."

"The North is my home," said the old lady, "and at its edge is the same great desert that surrounds this Land of Oz. I'm afraid, my dear, you will have to live with us."

"*Fuuuuuuuuuuuuuuuuuuuuuck*," I moaned. This wasn't like the movie at all. "*Fuck fuck fuck fuck fuck.*"

All this cursing seemed to concern the Munchkin guys, who all pulled out their handkerchiefs and kind of just stood there *fretting*. As for the little old lady, she took off her pointy hat, balanced the end of it on the tip of her nose, and counted to three.

The hat disappeared, and was replaced with a small chalkboard in the blink of an eye. The whole thing was goofy as hell, but the special effects were *amazing*.

She took the slate off her nose and read it aloud. "Let Dorothy go to the City of Emeralds," she said. "Is your name Dorothy, my dear?"

I sighed. "Absolutely."

"Then you must go to the City of Emeralds. Perhaps Oz will help you."

"Yes! Oz! The wizard! Was I not making myself clear?"

She ignored my tone. "It is exactly in the center of the country, and is ruled by Oz, the Great Wizard I told you of."

"Ugh. Okay."

"You must walk there. It is a long journey, through a country that is sometimes pleasant and sometimes dark and terrible. However, I will use all the magic arts I know of to keep you from harm."

"You're a hundred percent sure that you can't just, like, *teleport* me there?"

"No, I cannot do that," she replied, "but I will give you my kiss, and no one will dare injure a person who has been kissed by the Witch of the North."

"Whoa, whoa, whoa." It wasn't that I was freaked out just by the idea of kissing a woman. Madeline and I had actually tried making out once when we were thirteen, just to see if either of us was gay (it didn't do much anything for me, for the record, but Madeline liked it KIND OF A LOT). Remember, though, this wasn't the overly made-up but-vaguely attractive 1930s glamor model Good Witch of the North. This was a wrinkled, gray-haired old lady witch, and I was a *fifteen-year-old girl*. "What *exactly* do you mean by 'give me your kiss'?"

She came close and kissed me gently on the forehead, which, I would later discover, left a round, shining mark.

"The road to the City of Emeralds is paved with yellow brick," said the Witch, "so you cannot miss it. When you get to Oz, do not be afraid of him, but tell your story and ask him to help you. Goodbye, my dear."

The three Munchkins bowed low to her and wished her a pleasant journey, and then just left, walking away through the trees. The Witch gave me a nod, whirled around on her left heel three times, and straight-up disappeared into thin air. Toto started barking like crazy. To be honest, it freaked me out a bit, too. That didn't seem like an effect you could manage *with a community theater actor in the back of a mall store.*

What the *fuck* had just happened?

CHAPTER III.

HOW ARABELLA SAVED THE SCARECROW.

H ologrograms, I decided. *It was all done with holograms.* Then again, I had definitely felt the old woman's wrinkly lips on my forehead when she'd kissed me. Could they be *robots*? Was it like that one HBO show, with the cowboys? The one I don't watch? Because it looks stupid?

I looked down at the dog. "What do you think, Toto? Are you a *robot*?"

Toto barked. Of course, the robot theory couldn't explain the old woman's disappearing act, or that business with her hat turning into a chalkboard. Which left two possibilities, neither of them particularly appealing: some kind of drug-induced hallucination, or, I don't know, the fucking *Matrix*.

My belly let out a growl. If the magical land of Oz was all in my head, then my stomach was definitely in on the con. *Why didn't I get that damned corn dog?* I went back to the shack and rummaged through the cabinets to discover some bread and butter, which beat starving to death, at least. I ate some of it and fed some to the dog. Some nearby trees also had borne a variety of juicy and vaguely delicious-looking fruits, but I wasn't about to take that risk. This place was already proving very different from the movie I'd watched over and over in my youth, and at this point I was about ninety percent sure that random dangling fruit would turn out to be some kind of trap.

I stuffed the rest of the bread into a basket along with my old sneakers—if I had to walk all the way to the City of Emeralds, I wasn't about to do it without magical witch repellent, or whatever it was the shoes did in this story. They were surprisingly comfortable to walk in, too, although they did make an annoying sort of tinkling noise the moment they hit yellow brick.

But it's not like that would get annoying at all, since it was only like a SEVEN HUNDRED MILLION HOUR WALK BEFORE I EVEN GOT OUT OF MUNCHKINLAND.

They don't tell you that in the movie. They just cut straight to the scene with the scarecrow. But I walked and walked and walked, and there were vast expanses of farmland, picturesque as balls, but no scarecrows. Every once in a while I'd pass a domed blue house, and the people inside would come out to stare. I'd be all like, "DO YOU HAVE LIKE A HORSE AND BUGGY OR SOMETHING, I NEED A GODDAMN RIDE," but they'd just wave and bow a lot. Munchkins are super into bowing.

Seriously, though, that road went forever. Somewhere past the eight hour mark my phone went dead from repeatedly checking the time, and I had a disturbing thought. I hadn't started walking in the middle of a spirally Munchkin town center or anything.

Had I been going the wrong direction down the Yellow Brick Road this entire time?

The movie had made it seem like the whole trip through Oz was like a one-day thing, but apparently that was not the case. Now it was starting to get dark, and I hadn't even stumbled across my first song and dance number.

As if on cue, fiddle music erupted from somewhere up the road. I hoped this meant I would finally find that goddamn scarecrow, but it turned out that a particularly wealthy Munchkin was throwing a party to celebrate my unintentional witch murder. His name was Boq, and he owned what was by far the largest tiny blue house I had seen so far. People were dancing and laughing, and at least five Munchkins were playing fiddles. He invited me to join the feast and spend the night.

A big table on the lawn was loaded with pastries and cakes and fruit and nuts and all kinds of amazing-looking food. All I had eaten all day was the bread, and the dog had actually eaten most of it. I was RAVENOUS.

I looked at the food, though, and the over-eager Munchkins beckoning me to partake of it. Wasn't there some deal with food in fairy tales? Like, if you eat the food you're stuck there forever, or get turned into a goat or something? The *Wizard of Oz* movie obviously differed quite a bit from the book—for all I knew, that whole don't-eat-magic-fairy-food thing *came* from the literature I was currently voyaging through.

Also, I had been walking *all day*, and the theory that this whole thing was some low-rent theater production had been shot to hell within the first couple of miles. I was either being subjected to an elaborate simulation generated by some combination of *Star Trek* technology and hallucinogens, or *I had actually been transported to a magical land.* Either way, there must be secret rules that governed all of this, and I wasn't about to let some fairy lure me into a deadly trap just because I was—

"Oh my God, is that a *meat pie*?"

Fuck it. In retrospect, I'm pretty sure those things had some kind of enchantment on them, too, because I devoured like eight of them and I was still like, "WHERE DO YOU KEEP THE REST OF THE MEAT PIES?"

My Munchkin host just laughed. "You must be a great sorceress," he said.

"What? Why?"

"Because you wear silver shoes and have killed the Wicked Witch," he said. "Besides, you have white in your frock, and only witches and sorceresses wear white."

I was wearing a black hoodie and jeans. "What are you even *talking* about?"

"Your attire," Boq insisted. "It is kind of you to wear that. Blue is the color of the Munchkins, and white is the witch color. So we know you are a friendly witch."

I flipped over the empty silver pie tray and checked myself out in its gleaming surface. Sure enough, staring back at me was a cherubic-looking ten-year-old girl in a blue and white checkered dress. Judy Garland was actually around my age when she got the part in *The Wizard of Oz*, but evidently the real Dorothy was quite a bit younger. Also, her face was *slathered* in beef gravy.

Munchkin dancing and fiddle music actually get old pretty quick, so I was ready to retire as soon as the meat-sleepies kicked in. Boq showed me to a cozy room with a bed that was only about a foot too short for me. The mattress was soft, though, and I was exhausted. I slept soundly until morning, with Toto curled up on a little blue rug beside me.

At breakfast I watched a tiny Munchkin baby play with Toto—he was quite the curiosity, since I guess they don't have dogs in Oz. I was pretty sure that kid was going to get herself bitten, too, because she kept yanking the dog's tail, but Toto seemed to have far more patience with this whole thing than I did.

"So, like, how *far* is the Emerald City?" I asked.

"I do not know," Boq answered gravely, "for I have never been there. It is better for people to keep away from Oz, unless they have business with him. But it is a long way, and it will take you many days. The country here is rich and pleasant, but you must pass through rough and dangerous places before you reach the end of your journey."

Awesome. At least he was able to confirm that I was headed in the right direction. Also, I think he was a little bit afraid of me, because he had apparently made his cooks stay up late baking meat pies. They filled my basket and sent me on my way.

Several miles later, I was resigning myself to another exhausting day of majestic countryside and slipper blisters, when I finally saw it. In a cornfield not far off the road, stuck up on a pole, was a scarecrow.

This wasn't some pleasant-looking actor in a suit, though, with oddly charming burlap neck-fold makeup. This was, like, a *real* scarecrow, with a sack for a head that had been hastily painted with kind of a half-ass grimace to scare off birds. It was wearing worn-out blue Munchkin clothes complete with pointy hat, and stuffed with straw that left its entire body lumpy and misshapen.

I stared into its dead eyes. Was it possible that this was just a normal, un-enchanted scarecrow? "Uh, do you... *speak*?"

"Certainly," answered the Scarecrow, in a surprisingly husky voice. "How do you do?"

Aaaaaaaaaaaaaaagh. The overall effect was *terrifying.* "Fine," I murmured. AAAAAAAAAAAAAAAAAGH. "Uh, how do *you* do?"

"I'm not feeling well," said the Scarecrow, his painted mouth curling into a wide smile. "For it is very tedious being perched up here night and day to scare away crows."

"Yeah," was all I managed to mutter over the sound of my own internal screaming. "Sucks."

"Alas," he said, "this pole is stuck up my back. If you will please take away the pole, I shall be greatly obliged to you."

Okay Grimsbro, I thought, *suck it up.* Creepy or not, the Scarecrow was Dorothy's dearest friend in Oz, and obviously a vital plot point in this whole story. I reached up with both arms and lifted him off the pole—he actually turned out to be quite light. He also *wiggled* while I set him down. *Yeeeeeeeewwwww.*

"Thank you very much," the Scarecrow said. "I feel like a new man!"

As off-putting as it was to watch his painted-on scarecrow face speaking and contorting into various expressions, seeing him gyrate and move and bow and walk around on his own was somehow *even worse.*

"Who are you?" asked the Scarecrow, stretching, scratching himself and yawning. "And where are you going?"

"Go ahead and call me Dorothy, I guess? I'm going to the Emerald City to ask the wizard to send me back to... oh, let's just say Kansas." I was hoping he would at least be able to tell me how much farther Oz was, but the Scarecrow had never even heard of it. The city *or* the wizard.

"I don't know anything," he said sadly. "You see, I am stuffed, so I have no brains *at all.*"

"Ugh. So you're basically useless to me."

His uncanny, painted eyes lit up. "Do you think," he asked, "if I go to the Emerald City with you, that Oz would give me some brains?"

"Definitely," I said. "Or… *maybe*? At the very least a half-assed diploma or something that sort of *represents* brains. Which is better than nothing."

"That is true," said the Scarecrow. "You see," he continued confidentially, "I don't mind my legs and arms and body being stuffed, because I cannot get hurt. If anyone treads on my toes or sticks a pin into me, it doesn't matter, for I can't feel it. But I do not want people to call me a fool, and if my head stays stuffed with straw instead of with brains, as yours is, how am I ever to know anything?"

I was fairly certain that getting him to join me was imperative to somehow finishing this hallucination or video game or whatever the hell it was. Also, something about the way this horrifying nightmare creature truly yearned for more was genuinely touching. "If you come with, me I'll ask Oz to do everything he can for you," I said.

"Thank you," he answered gratefully. I managed to dodge his hug, but had to help him over the fence on the way back to the road.

Toto, for the record, was even more freaked out by this new addition to our party than I was. He kept growling, and stopping to launch into full-on barking fits.

"Don't worry about the dog," I said. "He hasn't actually bitten anything yet."

"Oh, I'm not afraid," replied the Scarecrow. "He can't hurt the straw. Do let me carry that basket for you. I shall not mind it, for I can't get tired."

Hmm. At least I wouldn't have to carry my own pies. "I'll tell you a secret," he continued as he walked along. "There is only one thing in the world I am afraid of."

I stopped in my tracks. "Oh. We're about due for a Wicked Witch sighting, aren't we?"

"No," said the Scarecrow. "The only thing I'm afraid of is *a lighted match*." He just stood there, staring at me.

Okay, *that* wasn't ominous at all.

CHAPTER IV.

THE ROAD THROUGH THE FOREST.

After a few hours, the road started getting rougher. Whatever municipality was in charge of yellow brick maintenance apparently gave fewer fucks the further you got from Munchkin Central. I had to keep an eye out for potholes, which of course the Scarecrow would invariably step right into, tripping and smacking hard against the bricks. It didn't seem to hurt him at all, but it meant I had to help him up while he laughed merrily at his own mishap.

And to be honest, earnest or not, I didn't really want to touch that guy any more than I absolutely had to.

Around noon, we parked it on the side of the road by a picturesque stream for some lunch. I didn't know how long my stash had to last me, so I endeavored to limit myself to half a dozen meat pies.

Partway through, I gestured at the Scarecrow with a half-eaten pie and kind of grunted.

He demurred. "I am never hungry. And it is a lucky thing I am not, for my mouth is only painted, and if I should cut a hole in it so I could eat, the straw I am stuffed with would come out, and that would spoil the shape of my head."

Once again: AAAAAAAAAAAAAAAAAAGH.

"Tell me something about yourself and the country you came from," said the Scarecrow, when I had finished my sixth pie and was eyeing a seventh, despite my pledge. So I told him about the mall, and how boring everything was there, and how the sales lady at the shop had basically tricked me into coming to Oz.

The Scarecrow listened carefully. "I cannot understand why you should wish to leave this beautiful country and go back to the dreary, fluorescent-lit place you call The Mall."

"Yeah, but you have stuffing for brains. And there's more than just the mall. You know, like cell phones and Netflix and Tumblr and junk."

I closed my eyes and clicked my heels together gently. *There's no place like cell phones and Netflix and Tumblr and junk.*

The Scarecrow sighed. "Of course I cannot understand it," he said. "If your peoples' heads were stuffed with straw, like mine, you would probably all live in the beautiful places, and The Mall would have no people at all."

"Fair enough," I said. "What about you? What's your whole deal?"

"My whole deal is very little indeed. I was only made the day before yesterday. What happened in the world before that time is all unknown to me."

Huh. For some reason I had assumed he had been stuck up on that pole a lot longer. "Luckily," he continued, "when the farmer made my head, one of the first things he did was to paint my ears, so that I heard what was going on."

"Wait, so was it, like, *magic* paint? Were they *trying* to make a living scarecrow?" I was just trying to figure out how he had come to life. "Did a talking snowman maybe give you that hat?"

"Not that I'm aware of." He continued his story—basically, the farmer had painted on his face bit by bit, chatting away with some other Munchkin, and the scarecrow had become more and more aware of his surroundings as he'd gone, but kept his mouth shut because he hadn't figured out how to talk yet. The farmer, for what it was worth, was crap at drawing faces. One eye was significantly larger than the other, and the ears weren't at all straight. After marvelling at their handiwork, the pair of them had hauled the Scarecrow off to the cornfield and stuck him up on the pole to frighten birds.

"I did not like to be deserted this way. So I tried to walk after them. But my feet would not touch the ground, and I was forced to stay on that pole. It was a lonely life to lead, for I had nothing to think of, having been made such a short while before."

It didn't seem like there had been anything special about his creation. Would *anything* with a face drawn on it come to life in Oz? I had a Sharpie in my bag, and thought about decorating a rock to see what would happen, but stopped myself. The thought of that rock, just sitting there, motionless, *thinking thoughts* for eternity made me shudder. If the farmer knew what he was doing, *the guy was a fucking monster.*

The Scarecrow continued his story. A bunch of birds had flown up, but they'd thought he was a real Munchkin and left, which made him proud. "By and by an old crow flew near me, and after looking at me carefully he perched upon my shoulder and said: 'I wonder if that farmer thought to fool me in this clumsy manner. Any crow of sense could see that you are only stuffed with straw.' Then he hopped down at my feet and ate all the corn he wanted."

"So the *birds* here can talk, too? Can they talk to anyone? Or just scarecrows?"

The Scarecrow, of course, had no idea. The one bird told the other birds he was a fake, and soon there was a whole flock feasting on his corn. So now he felt like a failure.

"But the old crow comforted me, saying, 'If you only had brains in your head you would be as good a man as any of them, and a better man than some of them. Brains are the only things worth having in this world, no matter whether one is a crow or a man.'"

So basically, some bird told him that brains would fix his problems, and that was enough for the Scarecrow. "By good luck you came along and pulled me off the stake, and from what you say I am sure the Great Oz will give me brains as soon as we get to the Emerald City."

"I genuinely hope he does," I said. The movie ended with some kind of vague platitudes about him having had brains all along, and then the whole thing turned out to be a fever dream back in a sepia-tone dustbowl. But they changed the ending of children's movies all the time. Like, in the original story, the Little Mermaid *dies at the end.* The truth was, I had absolutely no idea how this was going to turn out for him.

"Well, we might as well get on with it. Here, take my pies."

We continued down the road in silence. There were no more fences on the roadside, and fewer houses and fruit trees. The farther we went, the more dismal and lonesome the country became.

Something about the utterly arbitrary nature of his *entire existence* was upsetting me. Some farmer wants the crows to leave his crops alone, so he stitches together a *living being* with thoughts and feelings and *desires*? What if I hadn't come along? He would have just been stuck there for… how long did an average scarecrow last out in a cornfield, anyway? Would he have eventually just *rotted away*? All the time *yearning for more*?

I know it was all just a stupid story, but I decided that I was going to get the Scarecrow his stupid brains if there was any way I could.

Toward evening we came to a great forest, where the trees grew so big and close together that their branches met over the yellow bricks. The branches all but shut out what little daylight was left. I remembered being genuinely afraid of the dark, foresty parts of *The Wizard of Oz* when I was a kid. Also, I was pretty sure the Wicked Witch was in those woods somewhere.

"If this road goes in, it must come out," said the Scarecrow. "And as the Emerald City is at the other end of the road, we must go wherever it leads us."

"Yup," I said.

We ventured forth. After an hour or so the light faded away completely, and I was stumbling in the darkness. Toto seemed okay, though, and the Scarecrow insisted that he could see just fine, so he took me by the arm and led the way. The way his light, lumpy, wiggly arm pulled on mine made the whole experience that much more terrifying.

"Um, is there, like, anywhere we could stop and camp out for the night?"

"I see a little cottage at the right of us," he said, "built of logs and branches. Shall we go there?"

"Jesus Christ, yes."

So the Scarecrow led me through the trees until we reached the cottage, which was thankfully empty (or, the random sentient automatons that inhabited it were blissfully obscured by darkness, at the very least). I found a bunch of dried leaves piled up in one corner and settled into them to sleep, with Toto curled up alongside me to keep away the shivers.

The Scarecrow, who assured me he was "never tired", stood up in another corner and waited patiently until morning came.

CHAPTER V.

THE RESCUE OF THE TIN WOODSMAN.

When I awoke, the sun was shining straight through a sizeable gap in the cottage wall, and despite what I can assure you was a valiant effort, my attempts to screw my eyelids shut and ignore the daybreak proved useless. Somewhere outside, Toto was barking at birds, or squirrels, or Tooth Fairies, or whatever the hell they had in this godforsaken land. I sat up and looked around. The Scarecrow was standing patiently in the corner, eyes open wide, staring at me.

Aaaaaaaaaaaaaaagh.

My mouth felt like an ashtray and tasted like hate. "Ugh," I said. "Water. Does this place have running water?"

"Why do you want water?" the Scarecrow asked.

I'm generally grumpy on the very best of mornings, which this was very much *not*. "Um, to drink? To wash in?" I shot him a look that I'm not particularly proud of. "What the fuck do you *think* I want water for?"

For what it was worth, he seemed oblivious to my tone. "What is a *fugg*?"

As dedicated as I was to my crappy mood, his earnest, wide-eyed look of curiosity was too much. I cracked a smile. "It's not a fugg, it's a *fuck*. Like, you know, a bone? A shag? You can take a flying one at a rolling doughnut?"

He narrowed his eyes and nodded. "So a fugg is something that *flies*."

It was like he was constitutionally unable to say curse words. And, depending on what kind of simulation this whole thing was, that might be literally true. "It's a hard K at the end, not a G," I insisted. "*Fuuuuuuuuuuck*."

"Guuuuuuuuuck."

Jesus Christ. "Okay, starts with an F. FUH."

"Fuh."

"And ends with an UCK."

"Uck."

"Now say it all together."

"*Fluck*."

"Mother*fucker*!" That one was a real curse, not an instructional one.

"Futher mucker."

"NNNNNNNNNNNNNNNGGGGG," someone moaned from outside the cottage, loudly.

"I *know*, right?" The Scarecrow's mismatched eyes widened, and it dawned on me that, as far as I knew, we were the only two people in the vicinity. "Wait a minute, who said that?"

I poked my head out the door and heard another moan come from somewhere off in the woods. *Could it be...?* I pushed a few steps into the foliage, with the Scarecrow following close behind, and spotted something shining in a ray of that godawful morning sun. Sure as shit, next to a half-chopped tree trunk, with an uplifted axe in his hands, stood the Tin Woodsman. And here's something I was completely unprepared for:

The Tin Woodsman was fucking *hot*.

He wasn't all cylindrical and vaguely genderless like the guy in the movie. He was all sleek and shiny, like a *sexy motorcycle*. I don't know how they manufacture Tin Woodsmen at all, but his face looked like it was *chiseled* from something.

And, more importantly, he was *here*, which meant that I was that much closer to getting the hell out of this waking nightmare. Toto made a quick snap at the Woodsman's leg, hurting his teeth in the process.

"Praise Satan," I said. "I was worried we'd have to walk for two or three more days before we ran into you."

"If this Satan fellow sent you, then praise him indeed," the Tin Woodsman said. "I've been groaning for more than a year, and no one has ever heard me before or come to help me."

"Hold on. You can *talk* right now?"

"Of course."

"Then why were you *moaning*? For *a year*? Did it ever occur to you that random strangers might be more willing to investigate if you said actual words instead of making creepy sex noises?"

He stood silently for a moment. "I'm trying to shrug," he said at last, "but I'm rusted so badly that I cannot move at all. If I am well oiled I shall soon be all right again."

The Scarecrow ran back to the cottage to retrieve the oil can, and returned promptly. "So, uh, *which parts* get oiled, now?" I asked.

"Oil my neck, first," replied the Tin Woodsman. I did, but it was rusted pretty badly, so the Scarecrow took hold of the tin head with both his hands and moved it gently from side to side until it worked freely. The Woodsman let out a low, soft moan.

You're killing me, dude.

"Now oil the joints in my arms," he said. So we did, and the Tin Woodsman gave a sigh of what I can only call *satisfaction* and lowered his axe. "This is a great comfort," he said. "I have been holding that axe in the air ever since I rusted, and I'm glad to be able to put it down at last. Now, if you will oil the joints of my legs..."

Right. Of course. *The legs.* The Woodsman's whole, like, torso unit was much more contoured than the one in the movie, and while I wouldn't exactly say there was a bulge down there or anything, the way he was put together made it look like there might be some sort of... *compartment*? Like there could be *attachments* or something inside. I'm just saying.

I tried to get through the oiling as quickly as possible, but of course his legs were even more rusted than the rest of him, so the Scarecrow had to wiggle them all around like crazy. The process left me queasy and aroused in equal measure. And then ashamed, of course, followed by embarrassment, since, intellectually at least, I knew I had nothing to be ashamed of. Then, somehow, *aroused* again? Possibly by the *embarrassment*? The whole thing was a giant puberty shit sandwich, and I can't tell you how glad I was when it was finally over.

The Tin Woodsman thanked us again for his release. At the very least, he was polite.

"I might have stood there always if you had not come along," he said. "So you have certainly saved my life. How did you happen to be here?"

"Oh, we're off to see the..." I remembered my public domain restrictions. "...Oz guy. You know, the great and powerful wizard? The woods got super dark, and I think we spent the night in your cottage."

"Why do you wish to see Oz?" he asked.

"I want him to send me back to Kansas, or wherever, and the Scarecrow wants him to cram some brains into his head," I replied.

The Tin Woodsman appeared to think deeply for a moment. "Do you suppose Oz could give me a heart?"

"Absolutely!" I said. "Well, technically I have no idea. But it can't be any harder than giving the Scarecrow brains, right?"

"True," the Tin Woodsman returned. "So, if you will allow me to join your party, I will also go to the Emerald City and ask Oz to help me."

"Come along," said the Scarecrow heartily, and needless to say I was more than happy to have him join the party. His timing was excellent, too, because just a short way up the road the trees and branches grew so thick over the bricks that we couldn't pass. But the Tin Woodsman set to work with his axe and cleared a passage in no time.

This time, watching him chop away from a safe distance, the impure thoughts flowed freely without any of the extra baggage. *Yeah, that's the stuff.* In fact, after we continued our trek I was still so fixated on the way his hip joints rotated as he walked that I didn't even notice when the Scarecrow stumbled into a hole and rolled over to the side of the road. He had to call to me to help him up again.

"Why didn't you walk around the hole?" the Tin Woodsman asked.

"I don't know enough," replied the Scarecrow cheerfully. "My head is stuffed with straw, you know, and that is why I am going to Oz to ask him for some brains."

"Oh, I see," the Tin Woodsman said. "But, after all, brains are not the best things in the world."

"Have you any?" inquired the Scarecrow. Their whole conversation was weirdly polite, but nevertheless fascinating.

"No, my head is quite empty," the Tin Woodsman answered. "But once I had brains, and a heart also. Having tried them both, I should much rather have a heart."

"And why is that?" asked the Scarecrow.

"I will tell you my story, and then you will know."

"Hold on," I said. "If this is going to be a whole big thing, I'ma eat me some meat pies." I opened the basket and was a bit disappointed at how few were left. It was a good thing neither of my companions needed to eat, because there were barely enough left to last me the day. Toto wagged his tail frantically and barked, and I begrudgingly split the first pie with him.

"Okay," I said as we continued walking, my face half-stuffed. "Go."

The Tin Woodsman launched into his tale.

"I was born the son of a woodman who chopped down trees in the forest and sold the wood for a living. When I grew up, I too became a wood-chopper, and after my father died I took care of my old mother as long as she lived. Then I made up my mind that instead of living alone I would marry, so that I might not become lonely.

"There was one of the Munchkin girls who was so beautiful that I soon grew to love her with all my heart. She, on her part, promised to marry me as soon as I could earn enough money to build a better house for her. So I set to work harder than ever. But the girl lived with an old woman who did not want her to marry anyone, for she was so lazy she wished the girl to remain with her and do the cooking and the housework. So the old woman went to the Wicked Witch of the East, and promised her two sheep and a cow if she would prevent the marriage. Thereupon the Wicked Witch enchanted my axe, and when I was chopping away at my best one day, for I was anxious to get the new house and my wife as soon as possible, the axe slipped all at once and cut off my left leg."

"Jesus," I said. That shit just got *real*.

"This at first seemed a great misfortune, for I knew a one-legged man could not do very well as a wood-chopper. So I went to a tinsmith and had him make me a new leg out of tin. The leg worked very well, once I was used to it."

I have to admit, I was impressed by his can-do attitude. I almost asked how he even got to the tinsmith, but I remembered the sheer quantity of witch blood splattered all over the landscape a couple of days back when the house first dropped, and decided I was better off not knowing the gory details.

The Woodsman continued his story. "But my action angered the Wicked Witch of the East, for she had promised the old woman I should not marry the pretty Munchkin girl. When I began chopping again, my axe slipped and cut off my right leg."

Okay. I was starting to see how this was going to go down.

"Again I went to the tinsmith, and again he made me a leg out of tin. After this the enchanted axe cut off my arms, one after the other; but, nothing daunted, I had them replaced with tin ones. The Wicked Witch then made the axe slip and cut off my head, and at first I thought that was the end of me. But the tinsmith happened to come along, and he made me a new head out of tin."

"Sure," I said. "Why not?" If some random straw-filled burlap sack could walk and talk and have aspirations, why not a metal head? I reminded myself to never construct anything that even remotely looked like it had a face while I was here.

"I thought I had beaten the Wicked Witch then, and I worked harder than ever, but I little knew how cruel my enemy could be. She thought of a new way to kill my love for the beautiful Munchkin maiden, and made my axe slip again, so that it cut right through my body, splitting me into two halves. Once more the tinsmith came to my help and made me a body of tin, fastening my tin arms and legs and head to it, by means of joints, so that I could move around as well as ever."

Okay, who the hell was this tinsmith guy? I was beginning to think maybe we should be following whatever color of road led to *him*.

"But, alas! I had now no heart, so that I lost all my love for the Munchkin girl, and did not care whether I married her or not. I suppose she is still living with the old woman, waiting for me to come after her.

"My body shone so brightly in the sun that I felt very proud of it and it did not matter now if my axe slipped, for it could not cut me. There was only one danger—that my joints would rust. But I kept an oil can in my cottage and took care to oil myself whenever I needed it. However, there came a day when I forgot to do this, and, being caught in a rainstorm, before I thought of the danger, my joints had rusted, and I was left to stand in the woods until you came to help me.

"It was a terrible thing to undergo, but during the year I stood there I had time to think that the greatest loss I had known was the loss of my heart. While I was in love I was the happiest man on earth; but no one can love who has not a heart, and so I am resolved to ask Oz to give me one. If he does, I will go back to the Munchkin maiden and marry her."

Oh my God. *He was so emo.*

"All the same," said the Scarecrow, "I shall ask for brains instead of a heart. For a fool would not know what to do with a heart if he had one."

"I shall take the heart," returned the Tin Woodsman. "For brains do not make one happy, and happiness is the best thing in the world."

Normally I would agree with the Scarecrow—I'll take thoughts over feelings any day of the week. But at this point I was in it *deep* for that sleek, shiny, heartbroken son of a bitch. Even his *politeness* was somehow turning me on. I had to remind myself that both of them were probably some combination of computer program and drug trip, and regardless of whether they got their respective organs or not, the important thing was that I finish whatever the hell this was and get back home.

And soon. My stomach made a weird gurgling noise, and I quieted it with another one of the few remaining meat pies. They wouldn't actually let me *starve to death* in this thing, right?

Right?

CHAPTER VI.

THE COWARDLY LION.

W e walked on through the woods. By now the yellow bricks underfoot were almost completely covered in dead branches and rotting leaves, so travelling had become kind of a pain in the ass. Still, if this story followed the movie at all, I was pretty sure there was a Cowardly Lion somewhere in these woods, and once we added him to the group it was straight to Emerald City, one more witch murder, some tearful good byes and *bam*, back to the mall to fill out a VERY STRONGLY WORDED market research form. I'd be out of there in...

No time? I realized that I'd already been in the Oz Matrix or whatever it was for at least two and a half days. Was this one of those things where I'd wake up to find that no time had passed in the real world? Or was I actually laying on a cot in the back of a shitty mall store with wires and feeding tubes hooked up to me, and all of this was happening in *real time*? If I just never came home from the mall, my Mom would *freak the fuck out*.

Suddenly I was even more eager to return home. A deep growl came from some wild animal hidden among the trees. And even though I was specifically looking for something that fit that description, the little hairs on the back of my neck stood up.

"That was a lion, right?" I asked. "Do you guys think that sounded like a lion?"

The Scarecrow gasped. "I certainly hope there aren't any lions in these woods!"

I was definitely hoping there *were*. But come to think of it, in the real world, lions didn't even live in forests. "Um, how far are we from the Emerald City?" I asked the Woodsman. "Are there, like, any African savannas between here and there?"

"I cannot tell," he said, "for I have never been to the Emerald City. But my father went there once, when I was a boy, and he said it was a long journey through a dangerous country."

Well, that was no help. "But I am not afraid so long as I have my oil can," he continued, "and nothing but fire can hurt the Scarecrow. And you bear upon your forehead the mark of the Good Witch's kiss, which will protect you from harm."

Oh yeah—I had pretty much blocked that whole thing with the kiss out of my memory. There was another mysterious growl, and Toto scampered close to my side. This wasn't the kind of book where some animal *ate my dog*, was it?

As if on cue, there was a terrible roar from the forest, and an enormous lion bounded into the road. This wasn't some 1930s character actor in a fur suit, either. It was *an actual lion*, and it was *huge*. With one blow of its paw it sent the Scarecrow tumbling off the road, and it did its damnedest to maul the Tin Woodsman with its claws. He didn't even dent, but he fell on his side and lay perfectly still.

Toto ran straight toward the lion, barking, and the big cat opened its mouth to snap him up in one bite. It didn't look cowardly *at all*. Still, half on instinct and half based on the fact that I thought I knew how this story was supposed to turn out, I rushed forward. "*Please be the cowardly one, please be the cowardly one, please be the cowardly one,*" I muttered to myself.

Then I punched that big, stupid lion right in the nose. "DO NOT EAT MY DOG."

The lion yelped and fell back on his haunches. "I didn't eat him!" he whined, rubbing his nose with a paw.

Oh, thank god. "You ARE the cowardly one! Ha!"

"I know it," the Lion said, hanging his head in shame. "I've always known it. But how can I help it?"

"I don't know," I said, irked. Coward or not, if the Scarecrow and Woodsman had been regular people they'd pretty much be dead right now. "Maybe don't attack people who are stuffed with straw?"

"Is he stuffed?" the Lion asked, surprised. "So *that's* why he went over so easily. It astonished me to see him whirl around so. Is the other one stuffed also?"

"No," I said. "Tin."

"That's why he nearly blunted my claws," the Lion said. "When they scratched against the tin it made a cold shiver run down my back. What is that little animal you are so tender of? Is he made of tin, or stuffed?"

"Neither. He's a, uh… a *meat dog*, I guess."

"Oh! He's a curious animal and seems remarkably small, now that I look at him. No one would think of biting such a tiny thing, except a coward like me." He was starting back up with the self-pity schtick again.

"You get that it's not okay to maul people because you're scared of them, right? Like, straight-up *killing someone* is not an appropriate reaction to *the wiggins*?"

The Lion sighed. "All the other animals in the forest naturally expect me to be brave, for the Lion is everywhere thought to be the King of Beasts," he said. "I learned that if I roared very loudly every living thing was frightened and got out of my way. Whenever I've met a man I've been awfully scared; but I just roared at him, and he has always run away as fast as he could go."

"But that isn't right. The King of Beasts shouldn't be a coward," the Scarecrow said. He had managed to get back on his feet, and was attempting to pat himself back into shape.

"I know it," said the Lion, wiping a tear from his eye with the tip of his tail. "It is my great sorrow, and makes my life very unhappy. But whenever there is danger, my heart begins to beat fast."

"Perhaps you have heart disease," said the Tin Woodsman.

"It may be," said the Lion.

"If you have, you ought to be glad, for it proves you have a heart. For my part, I have no heart; so I cannot have heart disease."

"You know," I said, "that actually doesn't even sound like cowardice. It sounds like *social anxiety*. My friend Madeline has that. Pretty much *everyone* has that. What you should do is go to the Wizard and ask him to give you some Klonopin."

"And that would cure me?" the Lion asked. "Do you think Oz could give me this Klonopin?"

"Just as easily as he could give me brains," the Scarecrow said.

"Or give me a heart," added the Tin Woodsman.

"Then, if you don't mind, I'll go with you," said the Lion. "For my life is simply unbearable without a bit of courage."

At last, our little group was complete. Or I hoped it was, at least. For all I knew the movie had trimmed its cast for budget reasons, and the book version of Dorothy also teamed up with a talking broom handle and a motherfucking *pirate ghost*.

The dark forest, for its part, just kept going and going for hours. At least having a full-sized lion at our side seemed to be keeping miscellaneous hidden growly things away. The rest of the day was utterly uneventful. In fact, the most interesting thing that happened was when the Tin Woodsman stepped on a bug, and was so upset about it that he cried his jaw shut. Then he couldn't talk, so had to do a kind of frantic, grunting pantomime until the Scarecrow finally figured out what his deal was and got some oil up in there.

"This will serve me a lesson, to look where I step," the Woodsman said. "For if I should kill another bug or beetle I should surely cry again, and crying rusts my jaws so that I cannot speak." He spent the rest of the afternoon carefully walking with his eyes fixed on the road, meticulously stepping over every ant.

"You people with hearts have something to guide you," he said, "and need never do wrong. But I have no heart, and so I must be very careful.

When Oz gives me a heart, I needn't mind so much."

Of course, I had technically killed one witch already, and if the Cowardly Lion reacted to most strangers the way he had when he'd met us, he probably had a whole cave full of Munchkin bones hidden somewhere in the forest. If it was kindness the Tin Woodsman was after, an actual, physical heart didn't seem to have all that much to do with it.

I couldn't bear to bring it up, though, because I was sure it would break whatever mechanism that big, dumb robotic sweetheart was using as a substitute.

THE JOURNEY TO
THE GREAT OZ.

We still hadn't made it out of the forest when night fell, and with no convenient abandoned cottages nearby, we were forced to camp out under a big tree. The Woodsman quickly chopped up a big pile of firewood, and was amazed when I showed him how a Bic lighter worked. (I don't smoke, but carry a lighter regardless, because Peacoat Pete Zamora smokes, and somehow never seems to have any way to light a cigarette on his own.)

The resulting campfire was toasty and warm, and I sat down on a log beside it and shared the last of the meat pies with Toto. I was pretty concerned with what we would do the following morning for breakfast.

"If you wish," said the Lion, "I will go into the forest and kill a deer for you. You can roast it by the fire, since your tastes are so peculiar that you prefer cooked food, and then you will have a very good breakfast."

"Don't!" the Tin Woodsman begged. "Please don't. I should certainly weep if you killed a poor deer, and then my jaws would rust again."

So the Lion went into the forest and found his own supper—we never asked him what it was, and he never volunteered it. Meanwhile, I was trying to figure out how I could revisit the subject with him discreetly and—more importantly—cook an entire deer over a campfire by morning without the Tin Woodsman finding out.

Meanwhile, the Scarecrow had found a tree full of nuts and was filling my basket with them. Granted, his stuffed hands were so clumsy and the nuts were so small that he dropped almost as many as he managed to get in the basket. But the Scarecrow didn't mind how long his task took, since it kept him well away from the fire.

I nibbled on a nut that had rolled nearby, and found that it was actually quite tasty. They would certainly make an easier and less gruesome breakfast than fresh venison, and the whole basket full could potentially last me for days.

A short time later, when I was trying to build some kind of makeshift bed in a patch of dirt, the Scarecrow risked coming close to the fire to bring me a few big armfuls of dried leaves, covering me with them to keep me warm and snug. All of this lent credence to my theory that human hearts were vastly overrated.

It was surprisingly comfortable, and I slept like a rock until morning.

When daybreak came I found a brook to wash my face in, feasted on my bounty of tree nuts, and gathered the troops for the day's march. Alas, boredom was *not* destined to be our biggest problem on that particular day. About an hour up the road we came to a long, wide ditch that divided the forest as far as we could see on either side. It was crazy deep, and littered with jagged rocks at the bottom. The sides were much too steep to climb down.

Damn it. This part was not in the movie *at all*. "Okay, what now?"

"I haven't the faintest idea," the Tin Woodsman said. The Lion just shook his shaggy mane.

"We cannot fly, that is certain," the Scarecrow said. "Neither can we climb down into this great ditch. Therefore, if we cannot jump over it, we must stop where we are."

Astute.

"I think I could jump over it," the Cowardly Lion said, gazing thoughtfully from one side to the other and measuring the distance carefully in his mind.

"Then we are all right," answered the Scarecrow, "for you can carry us all over on your back, one at a time."

The Lion just gulped.

"I'll go first," declared the Scarecrow. "If you found that you could not jump over the gulf, Dorothy would be killed." I had forgotten that he still thought my name was Dorothy. "Or the Tin Woodman badly dented on the rocks below," he continued. "But if I am on your back it will not matter so much, for the fall would not hurt me."

"I am terribly afraid of falling, myself," the Cowardly Lion said. "But I suppose there's nothing to do but try. Get on my back and we will make the attempt." The Scarecrow climbed up on the Lion's back, and the big palooka walked to the edge of the gulf and crouched down.

"Why don't you run and jump?" the Scarecrow asked.

"Because that isn't the way we Lions do these things." Then, with a big spring, he bounded into the air and landed safely on the other side. It didn't even look particularly hard. I took my turn next, gripping Toto in one arm, holding tightly to his mane with the other hand. For a quick second it felt like we were flying, and before I had time to even be freaked out, we were safe on the other side. The Lion went back a third time and got the Tin Woodsman, and then we all sat down for a minute to give him a chance to rest. He panted like a giant, goofy Labrador retriever.

The forest was, if anything, even thicker, darker, and gloomier on the other side. I was honestly beginning to worry that we'd never get out of the damn thing. To make it worse, we soon heard strange noises from the depths of the woods that made yesterday's growls seem cute in comparison.

The Lion dropped his voice to a whisper. "This is the part of the country where the Kalidahs live."

"What the fuck are *Kalidahs*?"

"Monstrous beasts with bodies like bears and heads like tigers," replied the Lion. "And with claws so long and sharp they could tear me in two as easily as I could kill Toto." He gave me a glance that looked extra fearful, even for him. "I'm terribly afraid of the Kalidahs."

"Jesus," I said. "I feel like I am, too."

The Lion was about to reply when suddenly we came to another gulf across the road. This one was way too broad and deep for him to leap across.

"Thoughts?" I asked.

The Scarecrow looked around and tapped his burlap chin with an ill-fitting glove. "There is a great tree, standing close to the ditch," he said. "If the Tin Man can chop it down, so that it will fall to the other side, we can walk across it easily."

"That is a first-rate idea," the Lion said. "One would almost suspect you had brains in your head, instead of straw."

I was definitely beginning to suspect that the moral of this whole thing was going to be that your brains or heart or Klonopin or whatever was inside you all along, because it did seem like a pretty smart plan. The Woodsman set to work at once—as quietly as possible, because *holy fuck, Kalidahs*—and chopped most of the way through the massive trunk in just minutes. Then the Lion put his front legs against the tree and pushed with all his might. Slowly the big tree tipped and fell with a crash across the ditch, with its top branches on the other side.

So much for quiet. We had just started to cross the makeshift bridge when a sharp growl made us all look up. To our shared horror, we saw running toward us two beasts with bodies like enormous grizzly bears and heads like jungle cats.

"Kalidahs!" said the Cowardly Lion, beginning to tremble.

"RUUUUUUUUUUN!"

The Scarecrow, Tin Woodsman and I scrambled across the tree trunk as quickly as we could manage. The Lion, however, as terrified as he was, turned to face the Kalidahs, and gave a roar so loud that I almost screamed, and the Scarecrow fell over backward at the far side of the chasm.

Even the fierce beasts stopped short and looked at him in surprise. But they seemed to realize that they were significantly larger than him, and outnumbered him two to one. The Kalidahs again rushed forward, and the Lion hurried across the tree, his face twisted into a visage of pure terror. Without even slowing down, the big-ass bearcats leapt onto the bridge to follow.

"We are lost," the Lion whimpered, "for they will surely tear us to pieces with their sharp claws." His voice dropped to a whisper. "But stand close behind me, and I will fight them as long as I am alive."

"Wait a minute!" I said. None of this was in the movie I was familiar with, but *The Wizard of Oz* was hardly the only thing I had ever seen on TV. "Chop it down! Woodsman, chop the tree down before they can get across!"

Fortunately the trunk was thinner near the top than it had been at the tree's base, and the Woodsman managed to get through it just as the two Kalidahs were nearly across. The tree fell with a crash into the gulf, carrying the snarling beasts with it. Both were dashed to pieces on the sharp rocks at the bottom.

"Well," said the Cowardly Lion as we took a moment to calm our nerves and catch our breath. "I see we are going to live a little while longer, and I am glad of it. Those creatures frightened me so badly that my heart is beating yet."

"Ah," said the Tin Woodsman sadly, "I wish I had a heart to beat."

So emo, even with death staring him in the face. My own heart skipped a beat.

"Also," he said, my name is 'Tin *Woodman*.'"

"Huh? What did *I* say?"

"When you asked me to chop down the bridge you called me *Woodsman*. With an 's.'"

Tin *Woodman*. "Okay, that sounds like a porn star name. I'm not calling you that."

He didn't protest, which was good because I was far too exhausted to hear it. Now that I realized that riding on the Lion was an option, though, I did that for the rest of the afternoon. To our mutual delight, the trees finally began to thin as we progressed. By late afternoon we came upon a broad, swiftly flowing river, with the Yellow Brick Road continuing through green meadows, bright flowers, and luscious-looking fruit trees on the other side.

"That river looks kind of rough," I said. "Can we all swim?"

"Not I," replied the Scarecrow. "The Tin Woodman must build us a raft, so we can float to the other side."

Indefatigable as ever, the Woodsman (with an 's' in the middle, goddamnit) took his axe and began to chop down small trees. While he was busy, the Scarecrow found a tree full of fruit on our side of the riverbank, which was nice, since I hadn't eaten anything but nuts all day. I had *long* since stopped worrying that the local foliage was all part of some elaborate trap.

It turned out the chopping part went much quicker than the actual raft-building part, and night came before he could finish. We found a cozy spot under the trees and I curled up against the Lion's soft, warm, somewhat rank-smelling hide to sleep. The good old, reliable (still horrifyingly creepy-faced, but that was hardly his fault) Scarecrow kept watch over us, just in case any more Kalidahs came wandering all the way out to the forest's edge.

I dreamed about Madeline, Peter Zamora, Astronaut Ice Cream for some reason, and my Mom.

CHAPTER VIII

THE DEADLY
POPPY FIELD.

awoke the next morning refreshed and, to be honest, reasonably full of
hope that I was getting toward the end of this godforsaken literature
voyage, or at least to the part where we got to the city and were pam-
pered by leggy brunettes and blandly handsome guys in muscle t-shirts.
The Woodsman insisted that the countryside around the Emerald City was
beautiful, and as far as I could tell, the landscape across the river certainly
fit the bill. It looked idyllic as *balls*.

He was just finishing up with the raft (he didn't need sleep any more
than the Scarecrow did, and had been working on it all night, bless the
little empty compartment where he was supposed to have a heart). We all
climbed onto it, and the whole thing damn near tipped over when the Lion
stepped on board. But the rest of us stood up on the other side and just
barely managed to balance the craft out. The Woodsman and Scarecrow had
long poles, and started pushing the raft into the water.

It worked pretty well at first. But once we reached the middle of the river, the water grew so deep that the poles couldn't reach the bottom. The current here was swifter, and carried us downstream, further and further from the Yellow Brick Road.

"This is bad," the Woodsman said. "If we cannot get to the land we shall be carried into the country of the Wicked Witch of the West, and she will enchant us and make us her slaves."

"And then I should get no brains," said the Scarecrow.

"And I should get no courage," said the Cowardly Lion.

"And I should get no heart," said the Tin Woodsman.

"Yeah," I said, "and also THE PART ABOUT THE WITCH MAKING US HER SLAVES."

"We must certainly get to the Emerald City if we can," the Scarecrow continued. He pushed so hard on his long pole that it stuck in the mud at the bottom of the river. Then, before he could pull it out again—or let go—the raft was swept away, and the Scarecrow was left clinging to the pole in the middle of the river.

"Goodbye!" he called after us.

"Scarecrow!" I yelled.

"Oh, poor, noble Scarecrow," the Tin Woodsman sniffled as we floated further down the river and our companion fell out of sight. "The irony! Rescued from one pole, only to be left on another, to live out the rest of his days *abandoned forever*."

"We're not abandoning him forever," I said. "Also, dry your tears on my hoodie or something. He still has your oilcan."

"Something must be done to save us," the Lion said. "I think I can swim to the shore and pull the raft after me, if you will only hold fast to the tip of my tail."

He sprang into the water, and the Woodsman grabbed his tail. Then the Lion began to swim toward the shore with all his might. It looked like pretty hard work, but the raft was slowly drawn out of the current, at which point I took the Woodsman's pole and helped push the rest of the way to land.

We were all pretty wiped out (or, those of us with muscles and ligaments were, at least), and the stream had carried us God knows how far past the road that led to the Emerald City.

"What shall we do now?" the Tin Woodsman asked.

"We'll walk along the riverbank back toward the road," I said, "and hope we can spot the Scarecrow from the shore as we go." We moved as fast as we could, and even though I was pretty worried about the Scarecrow, I had to admit that the countryside was straight-up lovely. I mean, I didn't usually go in for all that lush, flowery bullshit, but these ones were so big and colorful it was almost hypnotic.

After what felt like hours, the Woodsman cried out. "Look!"

There, in the middle of the water, was the Scarecrow, perched motionless upon his pole, looking all lonely and sad.

"*Abandoned forever!*" the Woodsman cried. "Without *brains*, without *hope*, without even *the crows* to keep him—"

"Okay, ENOUGH with the abandoned forever crap! Lion, can you swim out and fetch him?"

"I'm afraid it would be no use," the Lion said. "Even if I had strength left to brave the river once more, my entire body save for my nose sinks below the surface when I swim. If the Scarecrow were submerged so, I fear the swift current would wash all the stuffing right out of him."

"Okay, he *might* be abandoned forever." I sat on the river's bank and tried to come up with some kind of plan while the Woodsman and Lion gazed wistfully at the Scarecrow. Eventually, some random stork flew by and stopped to rest at the water's edge.

"Who are you and where are you going?" the Stork asked.

Talking stork? Sure, why not? "Arabella," I said, too tired to waste any energy arguing with a bird. "Er, I mean Dorothy. These are my friends, the Tin Woodsman and Cowardly Lion. We're trying to get to the Emerald City."

The Stork twisted her long neck and looked sharply at the group of us. "This isn't the road," she said.

"I know it isn't the road!" Ugh. "We lost our other friend out in the middle of the river, and are trying to figure out how to get him back on dry land."

"Hmm," she said, craning her neck to look across the water to where the Scarecrow was perched. "If he wasn't so big and heavy I would get him for you."

"He's not heavy at all! He's entirely stuffed with straw. Barely weighs a thing!"

"Well, I'll try," the Stork said, launching into the air. "But if I find he is too heavy to carry I shall have to drop him back in the river!"

"Wait! Don't…" It was too late. She was off.

The big bird flew over the water until she came to the Scarecrow, then grabbed him by the arm with her claws and carried him back to the bank. When the Scarecrow found himself among his friends again, he was so deliriously happy that he hugged every single one of us, up to and including Toto.

"Tol-de-ri-de-oh!" he sang. "I was afraid I should have to stay in the river forever! But the kind Stork saved me, and if I ever get any brains I shall find the Stork again and do her some kindness in return."

"That's all right," said the Stork. "I always like to help anyone in trouble."

She seemed kind of great, actually. "So, how does this work?" I asked. "Do you join up with us now? Do you have any missing organs or personality traits you'd like to ask a wizard for?"

"I'm afraid I must go," the Stork said, "for my babies are waiting in the nest for me."

"Wait. Do you mean stork babies or *human* babies?" Storks were, like, the fairy tale euphemism for *childbirth*, right? "You know what, never mind. I don't think I even want to know."

"I hope you will find the Emerald City and that Oz will help you," the Stork said. Then she flew into the air and was soon out of sight.

We continued walking upriver toward the road. The sun was shining, birds were chirping, and huge flowers in red, yellow, white, blue and purple became so thick that the ground was more or less carpeted with them. The aroma was almost… *spicy*.

"That smells kind of good," I said. "Right?"

"I suppose," answered the Scarecrow. "When I have brains, I shall probably like them better."

"If I only had a heart, I should love them," added the Tin Woodsman.

His whole heartsick routine should have been wearing thin by that point, but to be honest I just found it endearing. I was exhausted and more than a little lightheaded from the overpowering flower smell, and just then all was right with the world.

"I always did like flowers," the Lion said. "They seem so helpless and frail. But there are none in the forest so bright as these."

There were more and more red flowers as we walked on, and fewer and fewer of the other colors. Before long the red ones had entirely choked the other flowers out. "Hold on a minute," I said. My eyelids were getting so heavy I could barely keep them open. "What kind of flowers are these?"

Poppies, poppies, poppies.

"It's opium! The spicy red flower stink is *opium!* Run, you guys! We have to run!"

I stumbled trying to move forward, so the Tin Woodsman and Scarecrow each grabbed me by an arm and pulled me along. I kept catching myself drifting off, and tried to jerk my head to force myself awake. It was okay, though, because I suddenly realized I didn't *need* to walk. I could just float along casually, and didn't even need to be afraid of the flowers, because every single one of them was wearing a miniature black peacoat and asking me if I had a light.

"Dorothy, wake up!" the Scarecrow shouted, severely harshing my buzz.

"It's fine, I'm not asleepy. Sleepytime… *good.* 'Sall *bermanerma.*"

"What shall we do?" asked the Tin Woodsman. I was still vaguely aware of my surroundings, but very clearly losing my battle with slumber.

"If we leave her here she will die," said the Lion. "The smell of the flowers is killing us all. I myself can scarcely keep my eyes open, and the dog is asleep already."

I wrenched one eye open and saw that Toto was indeed curled up in the flowers. I have to tell you that at that moment I straight-up envied the little son of a bitch.

"Run fast," the Scarecrow said to the Lion, "and get out of this deadly flower bed as soon as you can. We will bring the girl with us, but if you should fall asleep you are too big to be carried."

The Lion bounded forward as fast as he could go, and disappeared. The Scarecrow and Woodsman crammed Toto into my lap and kind of made a chair out of their arms, carrying me through the flowers as quickly as they could. We followed the bend of the river for a few minutes, and just as I was sure I couldn't stay awake a minute longer, we found the Lion lying fast asleep among the poppies.

The Scarecrow gasped.

"We can do nothing for him," said the Tin Woodsman, sadly. "For he is much too heavy to lift. We must leave him here to sleep, *abandoned forever*, and perhaps he will dream that he has found courage at last."

"I'm sorry," said the Scarecrow. "The Lion was a very good comrade for one so cowardly."

"No, wait, it's *fine*," I said through a yawn. The sleeping Lion looked to me like an incredibly comfortable bed just then. "The Good Witch saves us. Pretty witch… superimposed over the whole screen. Snow or… something. *All… goooood…*"

Consciousness deserted me at last.

THE QUEEN OF THE FIELD MICE.

'm not sure how long I was unconscious, but when I woke up I was laying on a grassy hill. I opened my eyes, and the sea of red flowers seemed to have been replaced with stubby brown ones.

Wait. *Those weren't flowers.* I blinked the sleep out of my eyes, only to discover that I was *entirely surrounded by mice.* Small mice, big mice, mice in every shade of brown, as well as black and gray and white. Literally *thousands* of them, and each and every one was staring up at me patiently with a little piece of string in its mouth.

What the *fuck* did I miss while I was asleep?

From somewhere behind me, the Scarecrow spoke. "Permit me to introduce to you her Majesty, the Queen."

Was I supposed to be able to tell which one of these rodents was *royalty*? "Uh, it's lovely to meet you… your Majesty?" I muttered, just kind of to the assembled mouse crowd in general. One of them made a little curtsey. Upon further inspection, I decided that she did look reasonably dignified.

"So, does somebody want to explain to me what's going on here?" I stood up carefully to avoid crushing the sea of rodents, and turned around to find the Scarecrow and Tin Woodsman standing next to the decapitated carcass of a big, yellow cat.

"Jesus!" That last part came as a bit of a surprise. "What the *actual fuck*?"

"I rescued Her Majesty from this ferocious wildcat," the Woodsman said. Now I saw that his axe was thoroughly coated with cat blood. "I have no heart, you know, so I am careful to help all those who may need a friend, even if it happens to be only a mouse."

"What about *the cat*? The cat didn't need a *friend*?" The whole thing seemed awfully arbitrary. I mean, the Cowardly Lion was off in the woods eating things that were probably at least as sympathetic as these mice were, and certainly much larger. I had been trying to convince myself that maybe deer and some of the other animals in Oz weren't sentient, and that the Lion was conscientious about which ones he made into dinner. But now I wasn't so sure.

"The beast had two rows of ugly teeth, and its red eyes glowed like balls of fire," the Scarecrow said. "Surely, it was a villain."

Okay. I was just going to have to roll with this one. "So now the Mouse Queen is our friend, and we're having a big mouse party. And the little pieces of string? What's the deal with those?"

"The Queen and her subjects have agreed to help us rescue the Cowardly Lion from the poppy field," the Woodsman said. "He is too heavy for the Scarecrow and I to move alone, so at first I thought we'd have to abandon him forever..."

"*Of course* you did."

"...but then the Scarecrow thought to build a truck from the trees by the riverside, and pull the Lion to safety by the combined strength of a thousand tiny mice."

He gestured to the river, and next to it there was indeed a sturdy looking cart, with wheels made from cross sections of a thick tree trunk. I remembered that it took the Woodsman all night to build a raft. *How long had I been asleep?*

"So, wait," I said. "You had to *decapitate* a forty-pound housecat to rescue these guys. But they're cool with carting around a full-sized *lion*?"

"I was concerned about this myself," the Mouse Queen said. Oh, good. It talked. "But the funny tin man assured me that he was a coward, and that he would never hurt anyone who is your friend."

He literally tried to maul us to death yesterday. I held my tongue. It seemed obvious to me that if the opium poppies knocked me out cold, they would certainly affect tiny rodents much more severely, and we'd quickly wind up with a sleeping lion AND like five thousand sleeping field mice. But my head was groggy, my back was sore, and I had an awful crick in my neck from sleeping on a goddamned hill.

"You know what? I'm just going to let this thing play out however it's going to play out."

The Scarecrow and Woodsman started fastening mice to the cart, using all the various strands of string that each mouse had between its teeth (I thought about asking where they'd gotten the string, but ultimately, who cared?). To my great surprise, it worked quite well. With the entire lot of them they were able to pull the cart easily, even with the Scarecrow and Woodsman riding on top of it (which, to be honest, I thought was kind of a dick move).

Fortunately, the Lion had almost made it to the edge of the poppies before passing out—I could see him from my spot on the hill. The mouse cart reached him quickly, and with a lot of grunting and groaning, the Woodsman and Scarecrow somehow managed to lift his huge, limp body up on top of it. At first, he proved too heavy for the mice to pull. But the Scarecrow and Woodsman helped push from behind, and they successfully hauled him out of the flowerbed and into fresh air before any of the mice succumbed to the opium haze.

It took an absurd amount of time to unfasten each little mouse from its tiny string harness, and to be honest the things kind of gave me the creeps, so I sat down with my back against the sleeping Lion and ate nuts while the others toiled away. It's not like we were going anywhere until the big guy woke up, anyway.

Each mouse scampered away once it was free, and the Mouse Queen was the last one to leave.

"If ever you need us again," she said, "come out into the field and call, and we shall hear you and come to your assistance. Goodbye!"

The Queen ran off, and I had to hold Toto tightly, because he started to chase her, and if I had learned one thing today it was that the Tin Woodsman would *chop your fucking head off* if you tried that shit. I hadn't quite decided if this bloodthirsty streak had made him less attractive to me, or more.

The Scarecrow went on a fruit run, and the rest of us chilled out by the Lion, waiting for his poppy trance to wear off.

THE GUARDIAN OF
THE GATE.

The Cowardly Lion took *forever* to wake up. When he finally did, though, he was overjoyed to discover that he had survived the flowers. After hearing about the mice and cart, his mood turned philosophical.

"I have always thought myself very big and terrible," he said. "Yet such little things as flowers came near to killing me, and such small animals as mice have saved my life. How strange it all is! But, comrades, what shall we do now?"

Something about his phrasing bugged me. *Comrades?* Was it possible that the entire point of this Oz business was to *indoctrinate* me in something?

We set out again upriver toward the road, and found it quite soon. On this side of the river, the yellow bricks were so well maintained they damn near shone, and it made for easy traveling. By then, though, my mind was going a mile a minute.

If this was all some kind of brainwashing trip, what were they even trying to reprogram my brain into? The first thing I'd done here was *crush an old lady to death beneath my house*, and everybody had seemed super excited about it. Then I met some folks, and we had to straight-up kill these big bear/tiger creatures, *purely in self-defense*, of course. Then the one guy who was LITERALLY crafted to appeal to my very specific (and, yeah, maybe kind of weird) taste in men, who cried his jaw shut when he ACCIDENTALLY STEPPED ON A BUG, just casually chops the head off a cat. *For the greater good.*

Holy shit, was I being *desensitized to violence*? Was I going to wind up a *mind-controlled KGB assassin* at the end of this? (Was the KGB even still a *thing*? Regardless, you *know* Vladimir Putin has people in charge of assassination and mind control, and I imagine there's a fair amount of overlap between the two departments.)

I had already decided that if Oz was just a crazy-advanced computer simulation, or some kind of drug-assisted guided meditation, or just my own screwed-up brain dealing with a serious head wound, the only thing to be done was to follow the rules, treat the whole thing as if I had actually been whisked away to an honest-to-God magical kingdom, and just hope for the best. But this new angle raised the specter of an altogether more sinister possibility.

The truth was, the closer we got to the Emerald City, the more reservations I was starting to have about murdering a second witch, and with *malice aforethought* this time. I mean, if it came down to my life or dumping a bucket of water on some asshole, sure. But I had the uneasy feeling that it wouldn't wind up going down *quite* like it did in the film.

As we walked on, farmhouses started popping up alongside the road, a lot like the ones back in Munchkinland, but bigger, and green instead of blue. A woman came to her porch to watch us pass, all dressed in green, of course. She took one look at the Lion and ran back inside.

"These people do not seem to be as friendly as the Munchkins," the Scarecrow said. "I'm afraid we shall be unable to find a place to pass the night."

Ugh. "Well, I'm getting pretty tired of nuts and fruit," I said. Also, poor

Toto refused to even touch the stuff, so as far as I knew he hadn't eaten anything since the meat pies, unless he had managed to nab himself a talking field mouse or something.

"Fuck it." If this was the kind of place where you could just walk up to someone's front door and ask them for dinner and a warm bed, it was at least worth a shot. I stopped at the next farmhouse and knocked.

A woman opened it just far enough to look out. "What do you want, child, and why is that great Lion with you?"

"The Lion's our friend, and trust me, he's more afraid of you than you are of him."

The Lion, for his part, looked mortified.

"So if that's the only thing keeping you from inviting us in, stop being Lion racist and get on with it."

"Well," the woman said after thinking it over, "if that is the case you may come in, and I will give you some supper and a place to sleep."

To be honest, I couldn't believe that it actually worked. But she brought us in and introduced us to her husband and two kids, and started setting the table while they just stared at us. We made some small talk, and I mentioned that we were headed toward the Emerald City to see the Wizard.

"Oh, indeed!" exclaimed the man. His leg was in a cast, and he was lying on a couch in the corner. "Are you sure that Oz will see you?"

"Pretty sure."

"Well, it is said that he never lets anyone come into his presence. I have been to the Emerald City many times, and it is a beautiful and wonderful place, but I have never been permitted to see the Great Oz, nor do I know of any living person who has seen him."

This was the part where the townsfolk go on and on about how intimidating the wizard was, to make sure we'd be suitably dumbfounded when he turned out to be some dude behind a curtain or whatever.

"He sits day after day in the great throne room of his palace," the man said, starting to get himself all worked up. "And even those who wait upon him do not see him face to face! You see, Oz is a Great Wizard, and can take on any form he wishes. So that some say he looks like a bird, and some say he looks like an elephant, and some say he looks like a cat. To others he appears as a beautiful fairy, or a brownie, or in any other form that pleases him. But who the real Oz is, when he is in his own form, no living person can tell."

"Weird," I said. "Still, I'll take my chances."

"Why do you wish to see the terrible Oz?" he asked.

"I want him to give me some brains," the Scarecrow said eagerly.

"Oh, Oz could do that easily enough," declared the man. "He has more brains than he needs."

"And I want him to give me a heart," said the Woodsman.

"That will not trouble him," continued the man, "for Oz has a large collection of hearts, of all sizes and shapes."

Ew. "And I want him to give me courage," said the Cowardly Lion. "Or Klonopin."

"I know not of this Klonopin of which you speak," the man said. "But Oz keeps a great pot of courage in his throne room, which he has covered with a golden plate, to keep it from running over. He will be glad to give you some."

All of this sounded like utter bullshit to me.

"But what do YOU want?" the man continued.

"Uh, to get back to Kansas, I think," I said. It had been a long day, and I had forgotten if I was supposed to play along with the whole Dorothy scenario, or if I could just tell people I wanted to go to the mall in Calabasas.

"Not you," the man said. "HIM!" He pointed at Toto.

Toto just wagged his tail.

We were finally called to dinner, THANK GOD. It wound up being scrambled eggs and a genuinely delicious porridge thing, with a plate of white bread. I devoured about three helpings, and Toto ate a fair amount as well. The Lion had some porridge, although he pissed and moaned about it because he said oats were food for horses and not lions. The Woodsman and Scarecrow didn't need to eat at all, but they were perfectly happy to keep chatting with Leg Cast Guy about all his absurd wizard conspiracy theories.

Afterwards the woman showed me to a spare room, and a bed that, after however many days on the road, felt like the *softest and most heavenly bed I had ever slept on in my entire life.* Toto curled up beside me, the Scarecrow and Woodsman went and stood quietly in their respective corners, and the Lion stood guard by the door. In close quarters, you could *really* smell him, too.

I had what was by far the most comfortable night of sleep that I'd had since I'd gotten there. I mean, it could be that I still had a touch of the opium in my system, but still. In the morning we thanked our hosts graciously and were on our way. I felt a slightly guilty about taking advantage of their politeness and pretty much forcing our way in there, but it had been a rough day, and my mind had wandered into some pretty dark places.

I was feeling better. I mean, still on guard against KGB brainwashing and whatever, but I was well rested, well fed, and ready to get on to the Wizard, on to the Witch, and finally get the goddamn hell out of Oz.

We started on our way as soon as the sun was up, and spotted a green glow on the horizon.

"Emerald City, here we come."

It got brighter and brighter as we approached, but apparently the city was MUCH farther away than it looked, because it was late afternoon before we finally reached the massive wall that surrounded it. It was crazy high, looked super thick, and was green as all fuck, just as promised.

I pushed the button next to the enormous, emerald-studded, sparkly green gate. I half-expected the guy from the movie to poke his head out of a trapdoor and give us a bunch of shit about not being allowed in, but instead the massive doors just opened.

We walked inside, and found ourselves in a big, high-arched room with even more emeralds stuck all over the walls. The interior decorators in this part of Oz were *not* subtle. A little Munchkin-sized guy standing next to a big green box addressed us formally.

"What do you wish in the Emerald City?"

I told him we were there to see the Wizard, and he was so surprised at my answer that he sat down to think it over.

"It has been many years since anyone asked me to see Oz," he said, shaking his head. "He is powerful and terrible, and if you come on an idle or foolish errand to bother the wise reflections of the Great Wizard, he might be angry and destroy you all in an instant."

Sure, he might. Granted, the movie I knew had already proven to be different from the original *Wizard of Oz* book in a lot of important ways, but I was fairly sure that the whole bit where Oz turned out to be a regular dude just trying to scare everyone was going to hold true.

The Scarecrow, however, was taking the gatekeeper's comments much more seriously than I was. "But it is not a foolish errand, nor an idle one," he said. "It is important. And we have been told that Oz is a good wizard."

"So he is," said the man, "and he rules the Emerald City wisely and well. But to those who are not honest, or who approach him from curiosity, he is most terrible, and few have ever dared ask to see his face. I am the Guardian of the Gates, and since you demand to see the Great Oz I must take you to his palace. But first you must put on the spectacles."

"Wait, what?" I said. "Why?"

"Because if you did not wear spectacles, the brightness and glory of the Emerald City would blind you. Even those who live in the City must wear spectacles night and day. They are all locked on, for Oz so ordered it when the City was first built, and I have the only key that will unlock them."

Once again, that sounded like a load of crap to me. But if we needed to put on sunglasses to get the plot moving, I was okay with it. The gatekeeper opened the big green box, and it was filled with green sunglasses of all shapes and sizes. He found a pair that would fit each of us—even Toto—and set the glasses carefully on our faces, locking them in the back with a miniature key that he wore on a chain around his neck. I wasn't thrilled about having something permanently affixed to my face, but if Gate Guy really was telling the truth, it was probably for the best. I knew myself well enough to know that if given the option, I wouldn't be able to resist a peek.

Once we were all bespectacled, the Guardian of the Gates put on his own glasses and was ready to show us to the palace. Taking a big golden key from a peg on the wall, he opened another gate, and we all followed him through the portal into the streets of the Emerald City.

CHAPTER XI.

THE WONDERFUL CITY OF OZ.

My initial reaction to the Emerald City was that the glasses didn't work for shit, because I was damn near blinded by the sheer gaudiness of it all. It was all marble columns and sparkly curtains, and there were emeralds embedded into EVERYTHING. Someone had Bedazzled THE FUCK out of that place. Like, if Elvis Presley and Liberace had a same-sex-marriage love baby, and sent it off to Donald Fucking Trump for style tips, the poor son of a bitch STILL would have been fired from his job decorating this place for being too understated.

I assumed that everything was painted green as well, although it was impossible to tell, considering that even the sun, the sky, and the skin on the back of my own hand looked green through my—

Sunglasses. Oh my god. *That was* the *whole point of them.* The goddamned Wizard must have said he was casting a spell to make the city green, then *locked tinted lenses on everyone's faces* so they wouldn't know he was full of shit. I mean, that was *way* worse than the mildly roguish snake oil salesman/balloon enthusiast from the movie.

The Wizard of Oz in this version was a fucking *dick*.

The Guardian of the Gates led us through the streets until we came to a huge palace dead in the center of town, which was somehow even more garish than the rest of the City. The door was guarded by a soldier with a green uniform and a green beard (or possibly not, because who could even fucking tell).

"Here are strangers," said the Gate Guardian, "and they demand to see the Great Oz."

"Step inside," the soldier answered, "and I will carry your message to him."

Well, that went better than I expected. He led us to a big waiting room (I'm not even going to bother describing the decor), made us wipe our feet, and politely excused himself to go announce our presence to his boss.

He took forever to return. "I spoke to the Great and Powerful Oz as through the door and gave him your message," the soldier said when he finally showed up. "He said he will grant you an audience, if you so desire. But each one of you must enter his presence alone, and he will admit but one each day. Therefore, you must remain in the palace for several days. I will have you shown to rooms where you may rest in comfort after your journey."

"Ugh, fine," I said, and turned to the Cowardly Lion. "The good news is, this guy *definitely* has social anxiety meds."

The soldier blew a whistle, and a girl about my age in a silk gown entered. "Follow me and I will show you your room," she said.

She had separate rooms for all of us, and mine was as tacky as you'd expect—velvet curtains, flowers in all the windows, and an honest-to-God marble fountain right in the middle of the room. There was a shelf of books (I secretly hoped one would be titled *The Mall in Calabasas*, but no dice) and a closet full of dresses that would probably fit the ten-year-old Dorothy just right.

"Make yourself perfectly at home," the girl said, "and if you wish for anything ring the bell."

"Ring, ring," I said. "I'm going to tell you straight-up that my clothes need to be washed *at least* twice. Also, send food—meat pies, if you have them. *All the meat pies.*"

"Of course," she said with a smile that actually seemed genuine. "You'll be fed at once, and your clothes laundered while you rest. Oz will send for you tomorrow morning."

The bed, at least, was plush as hell. After my pie feast I collapsed into it, but even with Toto curled up at my feet, I felt weirdly alone. It seemed I was actually growing accustomed to falling asleep with the Scarecrow staring creepily down at me, the Woodsman chopping away endlessly through the night, and the big, stinky Lion purring like a leaf blower.

Whatever. I was almost at the end of this stupid voyage through literature, anyway.

After breakfast the next morning (fancy toast and delicate poached eggs on a sparkling, hideous platter), the girl returned for me. She brought my freshly-washed laundry, which seemed to look like olden-time little girl clothes to her, even as she folded them into perfect squares—the physical logistics of the whole Dorothy disguise business continued to baffle me. Also, she really, *really* wanted to dress me up in stuff from the closet, but I refused. I finally let her tie a ribbon around Toto's neck, which seemed to satisfy her.

The hall outside Oz's throne room was full of women and men decked out in elaborate gowns and waistcoats, who evidently showed up to hang out with each other every day even though they were never let in to see the Wizard.

"Are you really going to look upon the face of Oz the Terrible?" one woman whispered breathlessly.

"Yup."

She turned to the soldier who had let us in yesterday. "Will he *see* her?"

"Oh, he will," the soldier said. "Although he does not like to have people ask to see him. Indeed, at first he was angry and said I should send her back where she came from. Then he asked me what she looked like."

"Okay," I said. "Creepy."

Now he addressed me directly. "When I mentioned your silver shoes he was very much interested. At last I told him about the mark upon your forehead, and he decided he would admit you to his presence."

Ah, so my witch connections were the ticket. That made sense. A bell rang, and everyone in the hall tittered nervously. "That is the signal," the soldier said. "You must go into the throne room alone."

He opened a door and I marched inside to a big, round, high-arched chamber. I'm going to go ahead and let you guess what every surface was embedded with. There was a big, green throne right in the middle of it, and floating about a foot above it was a giant, bald head. It wasn't even a particularly scary head. I mean, it was probably six feet across, but other than its size it just looked like a regular bald guy.

Its mouth moved. "I am Oz, the Great and Terrible. Who are you, and why do you seek me?"

The voice was loud, but not overly threatening. And I couldn't really tell if it was supposed to be coming from the giant head or from a speaker somewhere. I decided I should probably just play this one straight.

"I'm Arabella, although people around here mostly call me Dorothy. It's kind of a long story. I'm here to ask for a favor."

The head stared at me silently for at least a minute. Several wise-ass comments sprung to mind while I waited for him to get on with it, but I managed to hold my tongue.

"Where did you get the silver shoes?" he asked at last.

"From the Wicked Witch of the East, when my house fell on her and killed her," I replied. "By accident."

"Where did you get the mark upon your forehead?"

"A super-old witch kissed me there. From the North, I think? Then she told me to come see you."

Word on the street was that the Wizard could tell just by looking whether or not I was speaking the truth, and he stared at me like he was certainly trying. "What do you wish me to do?" he finally asked.

"Send me back to Kansas," I said. "And by 'Kansas,' I mean the mall in Calabasas, California. At the exact same moment I left, if at all possible. I mean, no offense or anything, but the Land of Oz kind of sucks."

I didn't *actually* expect him to grant my wish at this stage—in the movie he sends Dorothy to kill the Wicked Witch first, and then after she does he admits that he pretty much thought he was sending her to her doom, and that he's a phony who can't grant wishes anyway. But then he does grant wishes. Kind of. There's a hot air balloon involved, and Glinda the Good Witch has to swoop in and actually get Dorothy out of there. But I had already tried to skip ahead to the end once without any success, so I figured my best bet was to play along with the story as best I could.

His eyes blinked three times, then looked up and down and started rolling around independently of each other. To be honest, it was kind of freaking me out. Eventually, they focused back on me.

"And why should I do this for you?"

Because if you don't I'll expose your fraudulent ass to the entire, hideous green city? Blackmail probably wasn't the best opening move, I decided. And it was definitely WAY off script—if he felt like I was threatening him, shit could probably go real bad, real fast.

"Because I'm just a helpless, meek little girl," I said, trying to keep the sarcasm out of my voice and failing miserably. "And you're an all-powerful, super-manly Wizard Head who can grant wishes if he wants."

"But you were strong enough to kill the Wicked Witch of the East," he said.

"That wasn't on purpose, and you know it."

"Well," he said, "I will give you my answer. You have no right to expect me to send you back to Kansas unless you do something for me in return. In this country everyone must pay for everything he gets."

Awesome. He was a *Libertarian.* Also, he was full of shit. I hadn't paid for a goddamn thing since I'd been there.

"If you wish me to use my magic power to send you home again, you must do something for me first," he continued. "Help me and I will help you."

"Let me guess," I said. "Kill the Wicked Witch of the West."

"Kill the Wicked Witch of the West," he agreed.

"Yeah, I'm not sure I can do that."

"You killed the Witch of the East and you wear the silver shoes, which bear a powerful charm. There is now but one Wicked Witch left in all this land, and when you can tell me she is dead I will send you back to Kansas. But not before."

"If you want her dead so bad, *you* kill her," I said. "Unless, of course, you're asking me to do something that you're not powerful enough to do yourself."

"You have my answer," Oz said, "and until the Wicked Witch dies you will not see your home again. Remember that the Witch is Wicked—*tremendously* Wicked—and *ought* to be killed. Now go, and do not ask to see me again until you have done your task."

And that was that. Whether he wanted me out of the way and assumed the Witch would do his dirty work for him, or was just part of my KGB brainwashing (or, for that matter, he genuinely hoped to save his loyal subjects from the potential wrath of an old woman in green pancake makeup and a pointy hat), I had my marching orders. It was probably good that he was making us wait around a whole day between individual interviews, because I needed some time to figure out how I was going to play this.

I was led back to the sitting room, where the Scarecrow, Woodsman and Lion were waiting eagerly. "He won't help me unless I murder another witch," I said. It turned out they hadn't all heard the story about the first witch murder, so I had to explain that a little bit, at which point they were properly mortified about the Wizard's unfair demands, and did their best to comfort me.

Then I went back to my room to eat meat pies, flick green flower petals into the fountain, and think.

There was too much I didn't know about my situation—did I need to complete the book's plot to get out? If I went wildly off script, would I break the simulation? Would that be good or bad? And most importantly, if I died in the Oz Matrix, would I *die in real life*? I was still a little concerned about the whole brainwashing angle, but if that was their plan—"they" being the curvy, middle-aged librarian in the mall shop, I guess?—I was pretty sure it wasn't working. I wasn't going to kill anybody just because I was ordered to, and if they set up some shitty scenario where I had no choice but to do it, that wasn't on me, it was on them.

After breakfast the following morning, I was escorted to the sitting room again, where the Lion and Woodsman were already waiting. It was the Scarecrow's turn to see Oz, and apparently he had already been in there a good half hour by the time I had finished eating. When he returned from his audience, he looked a bit shaken.

"How was the big, giant head?" I asked.

"He appeared to me not as the floating face you described," the Scarecrow said, "but as a most lovely Lady, dressed in green silk gauze, and wore upon her flowing green locks a crown of jewels. Growing from her shoulders were wings, gorgeous in color and so light that they fluttered if the slightest breath of air reached them."

Okay, that was new.

"She spoke to me very sweetly, but insisted that she was Oz, the Great and Terrible, and demanded to know my name and my purpose."

"And I assume she told you to kill the witch too?"

"She told me that if I did, she would bestow upon me a great many brains, and such good brains that I would be the wisest man in all the Land of Oz. I was surprised that she required of me the very same task she did of you, but she said she didn't care who killed the Witch, as long as she was dead. And that once she was, I would have my wish."

The Scarecrow seemed even more bent out of shape about the prospect of witch killing than I was. By this point I had grown pretty bored of my room—posh-ass bed and all—so I spent the rest of the day poking around the city. I half expected to find some dark undercurrent beneath the glittering green façades, but none emerged. The people all seemed genuinely chipper, and thoroughly enamored of life in the Emerald City. So I swung by the gatehouse to make sure I wasn't technically a prisoner during my stay, but the Gate Guardian said he'd be perfectly content to take my tinted sunglasses back and send me on my way. If anything, he seemed like he'd be glad to be rid of me.

There was nothing to do but wait. The following morning it was the Woodsman's turn.

"I do not know if I shall find Oz a lovely Lady or a Head, but I hope it will be the lovely Lady," he said. "For if it is the Head, I am sure I shall not be given a heart, since a head has no heart of its own and therefore cannot feel for me. But if it is the lovely Lady I shall beg hard for a heart, for all ladies are themselves said to be kindly hearted."

"Dude, *really*? How did you lose your ENTIRE BODY in the first place?" I shot him tiny knives with my glare. "Shut up and go see the stupid Wizard."

Tin Woodsman did both, which gave me time to ponder the current state of my inappropriate robot crush. Well, inappropriate from *his* side, anyway—I wasn't about to apologize for the places my mind went when I gazed at his gleaming, mechanical hips. But I had to keep reminding myself that when he looked at me, he saw the same ten-year-old Dorothy Gale who was in the mirror every time I checked.

Obviously it had been lust at first sight from the moment I'd seen his rusted ass immobilized over that stump in the woods. And the endless pining for his lost heart—not to mention the almost eager way he was pre-pared to see his friends come to a poetically tragic end—still struck me as endearing rather than pathetic. Which was how I knew I had it bad. But something about the wildcat incident had thrown me for a loop, and I was trying to figure out what it was. I mean, he saved a helpless mouse (mouse royalty, no less) from being *literally devoured*. That sort of thing should have seemed straight-up *heroic*, right?

The thing was, any amount of cat-beheading, especially from a guy who cried his face shut when he *stepped on a freaking bug*, was a giant, flashing, neon-red flag. I decided that my misgivings came from the fact that I hadn't been awake to see him do it. Was he saddened by the horrible action the predator had forced him to take? Or had he done it with a little *gleam* in his eye, like cutting the heads off stuff was his whole deal, and he was excited that he finally had the opportunity?

When the Woodsman eventually returned, he looked shaken. "It was neither Head nor Lady," he said. "Oz took the shape of a most terrible Beast! It was nearly as big as an elephant, and the throne seemed hardly strong enough to hold its weight. The Beast had a head like that of a rhinoceros, only there were five eyes in its face."

"Yikes," I said. "Did he ask you to—"

"And five long arms growing out of its body! And five long, slim legs. Thick, woolly hair covered every part of it. A more dreadful-looking monster could not be imagined! Being only tin, I was not at all afraid, although I was much disappointed."

"Because you were hoping for the hot girl."

"I was, yes."

"And when he asked you to kill the Wicked Witch—"

"In a voice that was one great roar!"

"Right. Did he say you had to do it alone? I mean, is he pitting us *against* each other? Or did he say we could do it together, and have all our wishes granted?"

The Woodsman stopped to think for a moment. "No, he specifically stated that if I helped you kill the Wicked Witch of the West, he would then give me the biggest and kindest and most loving heart in all the Land of Oz."

Good to know. Now it was back to the waiting game. After one more PAINFULLY boring day, made bearable only by meaty, saucy goodness on demand, it was the Lion's turn at last. He had spent most of his downtime with the Scarecrow and Woodsman, trying to guess what form the wizard would take today.

"If he is a Beast when I go to see him," the Lion said, "I shall roar my loudest, and so frighten him that he will grant all I ask. If he is the lovely Lady, I shall pretend to spring upon her, and so compel her to do my bidding. And if he is the great Head, he will be at my mercy; for I will roll this head all about the room until he promises to give us what we desire. So be of good cheer, my friends, for all will yet be well."

"*Cowardly.*" Uh huh.

About half an hour later, when he returned from the throne room, I was engaged in what had become my favorite pastime over the last few days—

attempting in vain to teach the Scarecrow how to curse.

"Okay, repeat after me," I said. "Two tears in a bucket."

"Two tears in a bucket."

"Motherfuck it."

"Futher mucket."

The Lion burst into the room. "He was neither Head, Lady, *nor* Beast!" he said.

"You guys owe me five bucks each," I said to the Woodsman and Scarecrow.

"He was a Ball of Fire, so fierce and glowing I could scarcely bear to gaze upon it. The heat was so intense that I singed my whiskers!"

"And?"

"He said that if I brought him proof that the Wicked Witch was dead, at that moment he would give me courage. But as long as the Witch lives, I must remain a coward."

I had very much seen this coming, but I guess the others had been holding out hope for better news. "What shall we do now?" the Woodsman asked.

"There is only one thing we can do," the Lion said somberly. "And that is to go to the land of the Winkies, seek out the Wicked Witch, and destroy her."

My first thought was to ask what the hell a *Winkie* was, but I put a pin in it. The truth was, I'd had plenty of time to consider my options while loitering in the Emerald City, and I had come to the conclusion that there was no avoiding the Wicked Witch of the West. Of course, I wasn't in any way committed to assassinating the woman—if she was just some ugly old bat who the patriarchy had labeled "wicked" because she was tired of putting up with their shit, then more power to her. Maybe *she* would be willing to bargain with me for a ticket out of this dump.

But if she really was as horrible as everyone said—enslaving Winkies, bringing death and destruction with her everywhere she went, yadda yadda—well, then I'd cross that bridge when I came to it. The thing was, I had genuinely grown to like the Lion, Woodsman, and Scarecrow during our travels together. And, a little casual mauling and the occasional beheaded wildcat aside, they were three of the bravest, gentlest, kindest souls I had ever met. If the whole Witch thing went pear-shaped, I wasn't sure I could live with myself if I made a murderer out of any of them.

"I've decided to go and see this Witch for myself, and to make up my own mind as to whether she needs destroying," I said. "If any of you don't want to be a part of this, you don't have to come. When I return,"—*when*, I corrected myself at the last second, not *if*—"I'll tell the Wizard you all helped, and that he should grant each of you your wish."

"I will go with you," the Lion said without hesitation. "But I'm too much of a coward to kill the Witch."

"I will go too," declared the Scarecrow, "but I shall not be of much help to you, I am such a fool."

"I haven't the heart to harm even a Witch," Tin Woodsman said. "but if you go, I certainly shall go with you."

My own, stupid heart swelled up, and I got some kind of stupid emerald dust or something in my eye. "Then it's decided," I said. "We leave at dawn to the domain of the Wicked Witch, on the orders of some guy we barely know, who in all honesty, seems like kind of an ass."

There was a long pause.

"Futhermucking wizard," the Scarecrow said.

"Futhermucking wizard," I agreed.

CHAPTER XII

THE SEARCH FOR THE WICKED WITCH.

B ack at the gates to the Emerald City, Guardian Dude unlocked
our glasses and put them back in the box (without even spraying
them down like they do with shoes at the bowling alley—mine
were crusted with four days worth of sweat, and I can't even IMAGINE
what the Lion's smelled like).

"Okay," I said. "Which road do we take for the Wicked Witch of the
West?"

"There is no road," he said. "No one ever wishes to go that way."

Of course there wasn't. "So how do we get to her?"

"That will be easy," he said cheerfully. "She has but one eye, and it is as
powerful as a telescope, and can see everywhere. When she knows you are
in the country of the Winkies she will find you, and make you all her slaves."

"Perhaps not," the Scarecrow said. "For we mean to destroy her."

"*Maybe*," I corrected him. "We mean to destroy her *maybe*."

"Oh, that is different," the Guardian said. "No one has ever destroyed her before, so I naturally thought she would make slaves of you, as she has of the rest. But take care, for she is wicked and fierce, and may not allow you to destroy her. Keep to the west, where the sun sets, and you cannot fail to find her." I usually have a pretty good ear for disdain, but I genuinely couldn't tell if he was fucking with us or not. So I just thanked him and we headed due west, straight into an unplowed field.

The "green" bow Concierge Girl had tied around Toto's neck now looked white as the driven snow, which amazed my three companions to no end. I spent the better part of the morning trying to explain the concept of tinted sunglasses to them, but finally gave up.

As we trudged on through the afternoon, the ground became rougher and hillier. Also, there seemed to be zero trees west of the Emerald City, and I'm pretty sure it was *at least* twenty degrees hotter in that direction. I was exhausted well before sunset. The truth was, I hadn't slept much the night before, and even though I was so close to getting home I could practically *taste it*, I wasn't particularly looking forward to this next part.

I decided that we'd call it a day, and the Lion enthusiastically agreed, falling to his belly on the spot. I lay down and curled up against his already-snoring, stinky hide. After four nights in the softest bed ever, I figured going back to sleeping in the wild might take a little…

I was out like a light before I could even finish the thought. Alas, it was barely sundown when I was jarred awake by the sound of the Scarecrow's scream.

"WOOOOOOLVES!"

I scrambled to my feet in a half-blind panic, but slipped on the rough grass and fell. In the light of the setting sun, the Woodsman was attempting to calm his friend.

"This is my fight," he said. "Get behind me and I will meet them as they come."

From somewhere out of my line of vision, a low, rough voice growled. "The witch says that none of you are fit to work," it said. "So we may tear you into small pieces."

The Tin Woodsman seized his axe just as the wolf lunged toward him, and swung his arm in a wide arc, chopping the animal's head clean from its body. As soon as he could raise his arm again, a second wolf attacked, and also fell under the sharp edge of the Woodsman's weapon. There were forty wolves, and forty times the axe fell, until they all lay dead in a heap before him.

The Woodsman dropped his axe and fell to his knees.

"It was a good fight, friend," the Scarecrow said. The Woodsman turned his head and I saw that his face was a mask of grief, tears streaking down his cheeks. There was no secret, sadistic pleasure hiding behind that expression.

These were the lengths he would go to protect me.

I rushed to his side to wipe his face with my hoodie before he rusted, but he flinched at my touch. "Go back to sleep, my child," he said. "The Wicked Witch won't have expected her attack to fail. We'll be safe until morning."

"I, uh..." He clearly needed some time to himself. "I'll just go relax over there. Away from the... *pile.*"

"I'll come with you, to stand watch," the Scarecrow said.

The Woodsman nodded. "And I shall bury the bodies."

I went back to the Lion—who of course had slept soundly through the entire ordeal—but, needless to say, lay awake restlessly for most of the night. When dawn came at last, there was nothing to do but make a little breakfast of the meat pies I had squirrelled away in my basket and continue our journey.

We had barely walked an hour when a small, black cloud approached from the west. As it came closer, I could see that it was in fact a flock of crows, rushing straight toward us.

"This is *my* battle," the Scarecrow said, "so lie down beside me and cover your eyes, and you will not be harmed."

We did as he said—even the Lion, although I felt like he was big enough that he could probably hold his own against a handful of birds—and the Scarecrow stood up tall and stretched out his arms. The crows scattered, not daring to come near. Because, you know, they were *crows*, and scaring them was pretty much the Scarecrow's whole deal.

Alas, the crows had a king, who was apparently brighter and braver than the rest. "It is only a stuffed man," he cawed. "I will peck his eyes out."

The King Crow flew at the Scarecrow, who caught it by the head and snapped its neck with one swift motion.

Holy shit, that was badass. I mean, not as badass as decapitating wolves, but still. Another crow flew at him, and the Scarecrow twisted its neck also. There were forty crows, and forty times the Scarecrow twisted a neck, until at last all were lying dead beside him.

Maybe I really *was* getting desensitized to violence, or maybe crows just didn't warrant as much sympathy as big, hundred-pound mammals, but I wasn't nearly as shaken up as I had been the previous night. The Scarecrow, for his part, also seemed like he was pretty much okay with it. We left the pile of birds where it was and continued on.

The Witch had presumably been watching closely with her freaky telescope eye, because before long we heard a soft buzzing coming from the west.

"*Bees!*" I looked around at my companions. "Okay, which one of you guys is an expert at killing bees?"

"Not I," the Lion said. "I am allergic to bees! Or at the very least, quite afraid of them."

"Take out my straw and scatter it over Dorothy and Toto and the Lion," the Scarecrow said to the Woodsman, "so the bees cannot sting them."

"Okay, that can't possibly work," I said. "The Lion is *way* bigger than you are—how much stuffing is even *in* there? Also, I'm *pretty sure* bees can sting through straw."

The Woodsman was already grabbing fistfuls of straw from the Scarecrow's torso, however, and before long he had somehow managed to cover us completely. Evidently the land of Oz operated mostly on *cartoon* physics. He tucked the Scarecrow's head into my straw-covered arm to hold.

"See?" the Scarecrow said. I could feel his face *wiggling* as he spoke. "It's a foolproof plan."

Aaaaaaaaaaaaaaaaaaagh.

Sure enough, when bees arrived they found no one but the Woodsman to sting, so they flew at him and broke off all their stingers against his shiny metal ass without hurting him the slightest bit. And they were the kind of bees that couldn't live without their stingers, too, because they all fell to the ground, dead. When I poked my head out of the straw they lay scattered thick about the Woodsman in tiny little heaps.

We stuffed the Scarecrow back up until he was as good as ever, and started upon our journey once more. This time we walked uninterrupted for several hours, until we spotted a dozen men and women with long, pointed spears marching toward us.

The Winkies, I presumed? They just looked like regular men and women. In fact, as they got closer, they all appeared pretty scruffy and underfed. I guess their favorite color was yellow, because they were dressed in it from head to toe, although their clothes were tattered and torn.

The Cowardly Lion bounded toward them. *Oh, crap. Please don't kill the Winkies, please don't kill the Winkies.* Then I realized I could say it out loud.

"Lion! DO NOT kill the Winkies!"

He stopped in his tracks and let out a mighty roar. The poor Winkies were so frightened that they turned and ran as fast as they could, disappearing into the hills.

"Is it just me," I said, "or are these attacks getting lamer and lamer as they go?"

As if to answer my question, the sky darkened to the west, and we heard a low rumbling in the air.

"More crows?" the Tin Woodsman asked. As the dark patch of sky came closer, there was a rushing of wings, and a great chattering and laughing.

Oh, shit. *Flying. Fucking. Monkeys.*

Each one was nearly as big as me, and their massive, greasy black wings blotted out the sun. The flying monkeys were *terrifying*. Two of them swooped out of the sky and snatched up the Scarecrow, pulling all of the straw out of his clothes and head with their long fingers. They made his clothes into a small bundle and threw it into the top branches of a tree.

I'm not terribly proud of it, but I screamed.

Other monkeys threw lengths of rope around the Lion and wound the coils around his body, head and legs until he was unable to bite or scratch or struggle in any way. Then they lifted him up and flew away with him to the west.

Three more monkeys seized the Tin Woodsman and flew him high into the sky. I watched as they carried him toward a patch of rough terrain off toward the horizon, and dropped him to fall helplessly to the jagged rocks far below.

"Noooooooooooooooo!"

The biggest, ugliest flying monkey of them all flew toward me, his long, hairy arms stretched out and his face grinning terribly. At the last moment, however, he veered away.

"We dare not harm this girl," he said to others. "For she is protected by the Power of Good, and that is greater than the Power of Evil. All we can do is to carry her to the castle of the Wicked Witch and leave her there."

So, carefully and gently, they lifted me in their grimy paws and carried me for miles through the air to the witch's castle, where they plopped me right down on the front doorstep.

The Wicked Witch of the West didn't look anything like she did in the movie. She was small and decrepit, sported an eye patch, and wore her hair in big, rough braids. Instead of a pointy hat, she had a goofy golden cap studded with diamonds and rubies. She wore a big, heavy, wool coat, and a black skirt decorated with flowers, frogs and moons.

"We have obeyed you as far as we were able," the biggest monkey said. "The Tin Woodman and the Scarecrow are destroyed, and the Lion is tied up in your yard. The little girl we dare not harm, nor the dog she carries in her arms. Your power over our band is now ended, and you will never see us again."

Then all the winged monkeys, laughing and chattering away, flew off and disappeared into the sky.

Destroyed. It *couldn't* be true. I'd already seen the scarecrow emptied out and restuffed again, none the worse for wear. And the Woodsman... *he's tough*, I assured myself. I'd find him and hammer out his dents myself, and he'd be just as good as new. Right?

Right?

The Witch glared at me, then glared at my silver shoes even harder, and actually gasped. "Come with me," she said. "And see that you mind everything I tell you. For if you do not I will make an end of you, as I did of the Tin Woodman and the Scarecrow."

Fuck you, I thought. *Fuuuuuuuuuuuuck yoooooooouuuuuu.*

She led me through her castle—which was actually quite posh on the inside—until we got to the kitchen, where she told me to sweep the floor and keep the fire fed until it came time for dinner. The first thing I did—*believe me*—was check the sink, but there was no faucet, and it was dry. Evidently they carted the water in from somewhere else.

The Witch stormed off, leaving me alone. But I sure as hell wasn't going to hang around and do her janitorial work. I backtracked to the castle gates, only to find two sad-looking Winkie guards with spears blocking my exit. They may or may not have been two of the same ones we'd encountered in the fields earlier that day—it was hard to tell under all those tattered yellow clothes.

"Out of my way," I said forcefully. "See this mark on my head? Good Witch Kiss. If you even touch me, that shit will *mess you up*."

I had no idea if any of that was true or not. But the first guard just lowered his spear. "The Wicked Witch commands that we stop you from leaving, even if doing so will surely strike us dead. We must obey the Wicked Witch."

"Bullshit!" I said. "I saw you guys turn and run when the Lion roared at you. Just run away!"

The guard shook his head. "That was blind terror, and our bodies fled of their own volition, quite beyond our control." Now I could see that he was trying to hold back tears. "This is more of an… *existential dread*. If I try to stop you, and you strike me down, the next Winkie will and be struck down after me. And the next one after him."

The other guard—the next Winkie, apparently—just stared at me and shook his head in fear. *Jesus Christ.* Okay, maybe I'd go see if the castle had a back door. My plan was to get free, go revive the Scarecrow and the Woodsman, then come back, rescue the Lion, and figure out what to do about the Witch. I lurked through the corridors as quietly as I could—fucking Toto would occasionally bark at a Winkie patrol, but they mostly pretended not to see us and hurried along their way.

I eventually found an unguarded doorway into what appeared to be a courtyard. The Witch was there, waving a bunch of leather straps or something in front of a sturdy iron gate.

"If I cannot harness you," she said, "I can starve you. You shall have nothing to eat until you do as I wish!"

From the other side of the gate, the Cowardly Lion growled. "If you come in this yard, I swear that I will eat *you*."

The witch howled and turned away from him. "You!" she said when she spotted me sneaking up behind her. "Done with the sweeping, are you?" She glanced down at my shoes and grimaced. Then, suddenly, her face lit up.

"Well, you're filthy. Time for your bath! Go and get washed up, and then you shall have your dinner."

"My bath? Like, in a tub? Of *water*?"

"Yes, yes!" the Witch said. "The bath is on the top floor, just atop the stairs. You can't miss it!" She hurried back into the castle, giggling to herself along the way.

I ran to the gate, but it led only to a closed area, where the Lion lay, quietly weeping. The gate was chained tight with a massive iron padlock. "Hold on," I said.

He looked up. "Dorothy?"

"Yeah! Or, you know, whatever."

He leapt toward the gate. "I was certain she had killed you!"

"It's good to see you, too. I have to go real quick, but I'll be back! I'll have you free in no time."

I was pretty sure the Witch's plan was to steal my shoes while I was taking a bath, but if there was water in that tub… Well, a lot of things in this book were different than they were in the movie, but a lot of things were *the same*. And I knew *exactly* what happened when Dorothy dumped water on the Wicked Witch in the movie version.

I found the bathroom at the top of the stairs, and, sure enough, there were two big buckets of water next to the tub, one steaming hot and the other cold. I rushed across the floor toward them—and tripped over something, stumbling to the floor.

One of my silver shoes went skittering across the tile, and the Wicked Witch leapt from her hiding place behind a curtain, snatched it up, and put it in her own gnarled foot.

An iron bar, made invisible by some kind of spell, appeared on the floor. The witch cackled with glee. "Now half the shoes' charm is mine, and you cannot use it against me!"

That was her big, scary magic plan? An invisible *tripping hazard*? "Give me back my shoe," I said.

"I will not," she retorted. "For it is now my shoe, and not yours."

Now I was pissed. "Give me back my shoe, and set the Lion free, and let us both leave this place to go find our friends."

"Fool," she said. "I told you, your friends are dead."

"They're not!"

Her one eye opened wide, and wiggled around a bit. "I can see them myself! The Scarecrow's straw is scattered to the winds, and the Tin Woodman lays at the bottom of a ravine, smashed beyond repair. The spells that once animated them have been broken! They're dead, dead, *dead*! And once that charm on your forehead has faded, you'll join them, and your little dog, t—"

I dumped the bucket of hot water right on top of her head.

She gave a screech, and then instantly began to shrink and fall away.

"See what you have done!" she screamed. "Didn't you know water would be the end of me?"

"Of course I fucking knew."

She shrieked again, and I dumped the second bucket over her until she had melted away completely. This wasn't some special effect with a trap door, either—there was melted witch *everywhere*. I fetched my shoe, wiped the witch goo out of it, and made my way back to the courtyard to free the Lion.

"The Wicked Witch has met her end," I told him when I got there. "Also, I *might* be a mind-controlled KGB assassin."

CHAPTER XIII.

THE RESCUE.

The Lion was thrilled to hear the witch had been melted, and didn't understand the part about the KGB, so once I flagged down a befuddled Winkie to fetch his key, he was pleased as punch.

"If only our friends, the Scarecrow and the Tin Woodman, were with us," he said, "I should be quite happy."

Meanwhile, the Winkies were just about losing their shit. I hadn't heard a single musical number the entire time I'd been in Oz, but I could swear they were just on the verge of breaking out into a chorus of "Ding Dong, the Witch is Dead."

Several dozen of them had gathered in the courtyard. "From this day forward," one of them decreed, "We shall keep this date as a holiday to honor the one who freed us from bondage. The Feast of Dorothy!"

"The Feast of Dorothy!" the others cheered.

"How about the Feast of Arabella?" I said. "I just like the sound of it better. And before you start with the merrymaking, do you think you could help us find our friends?"

The Winkies were more than delighted to mount a search party. I explained that one was a bundle of clothes tied to the top of a tree near where the flying monkeys had captured us, and the other was made of tin, and possibly laying in the bottom of a ravine.

They sent their brightest and fastest to comb the countryside, but it was slow going. Fortunately, the Witch's castle was even more comfortable than our rooms in the Emerald City had been. Late on our third day, I was in the kitchen trying to explain to the cooks what a proper meat pie should look like (the closest they had come so far was sort of a pile of beef on top of a flaky pastry crust, which actually tasted pretty good, but would hardly travel well).

There was a sudden commotion out in the hallway. "We've found the Tin Man!" someone shouted.

I rushed out to greet them, and saw the Cowardly Lion bounding in from across the castle. Four Winkies tenderly carried the Woodsman in their arms, but he didn't look good. His body was battered and bent, and his eyes were open, staring, lifeless. A fifth Winkie carried his axe on her shoulder, but the blade was rusted and the handle broken off short.

I struggled to keep my composure. "In Munchkinland," I stuttered. "A *tinsmith*. A really good tinsmith…"

"Oh, we Winkies are famous for our smithery!" the woman with the axe said. "I'm sure we can straighten out those dents, and bend him back into shape again, and weld him together where he is broken! Give us time, and we shall mend him so he will be as good as ever."

They set up shop in a big, yellow room in the castle, hammering and twisting and bending and soldering and polishing and pounding the hell out of the Tin Woodsman. It was not quick work, however. Three more days passed, and four more nights, until a Winkie messenger arrived with news of the Scarecrow.

"We've found the tree at last!" he said. "Alas, it is a very tall tree, and the trunk is so smooth that none of us can climb it."

"Then I suppose I'll have to chop that *futhermucker* down," a familiar voice said from behind me.

The Tin Woodsman swept me up in a huge embrace, and he was crying, and I was crying, and the Lion appeared from somewhere and was also crying, and trying so hard to wipe the tears off the Woodsman's face with his tail that it became sopping wet, and he had to go out and dry it in the courtyard. The Winkie Tinsmiths had done excellent work. Sure, there was a bit of rough soldering, and some sections of him looked a little patched, but if anything, it made him look *rugged*. His joints worked just as well as ever, and, more importantly, he was his same old tragic, emo self.

He went on for several minutes about how he had been certain that he'd been *abandoned forever*, and the very specific details of his imagined destiny, broken to pieces on the jagged rocks. "But listen to me," he said at last, "wasting time when there is precious little time to waste! We must hurry to save our friend the Scarecrow, lest he should suffer the fate I have very happily avoided!"

Unfortunately, the trip was *much* longer by foot than by flying monkey, and it would take several days just to reach the Scarecrow's tree. "I shall make the journey alone," the Woodsman said. "For I can travel night and day without tiring, and cut the time in half."

"We shall post footmen along your path, and keep them well-rested, so you shall always have a fresh guide to lead your way," the Winkie messenger said. "The land around this castle has fallen to ruin, and in the bleak countryside it is treacherously easy to lose one's way."

The Winkies brought the Woodsman his axe—while the tinsmiths had been repairing him, other craftsmen had been polishing it, and fitting it with a handle made of solid gold. It was kind of nuts. Then he made his farewells, and there was nothing for the Lion and I to do but settle in and continue freeloading.

It was a *terrible* imposition.

After three full days, the Woodsman returned with the Scarecrow's clothes (including, thankfully, his emptied-out face sack, which was somehow looked even creepier than when it was properly stuffed). Now all we could hope was that whatever enchantment had brought him to life was on the cloth, and not in the stuffing, which was long gone by the time the Woodsman had reached him.

The Scarecrow's repairs were much quicker than the Tin Woodsman's had been—we crammed him full of straw from the Lion's bedding, and he bounded to life, good as ever. There were more hugs, more tears, and more wiping and soaking and drying of tails. The Winkies seemed every bit as delighted as the four of us were.

"Now may we begin the Feast of Arabella?" one of them asked.

"Yes, now you may begin the Feast of Arabella."

The Feast of Arabella, I have to say, was *raging*. There was music, and dancing, and drink, and proper meat pies that put the original Munchkin delicacies to shame. I have no idea how long the revelry lasted, but at some point I collapsed, only to awaken the following morning and discover that the festivities were still going strong. The Scarecrow and Woodsman, as tireless as ever, had partied straight through the night.

They took a break to join the Lion and I at our breakfast, and the Woodsman sighed. "I don't know about the rest of you, but I think I'd be content to stay in this castle forever."

It *was* a really nice castle. I considered the prospect. There certainly wasn't anything back in Calabasas that compared to this life of luxury, being waited on by grateful Winkies hand and foot. I thought about Madeline, though, and my Mom. The thing was, none of this quite felt *real*. And, although I loved my new friends as much as I loved the characters in a really good book, I couldn't avoid the feeling that they weren't real either. Not *really*.

The thought came with a pang of loneliness. "I think we have to go back to the Emerald City," I said. "And make that Wizard pay up."

"Yes," the Woodsman said. "At last I shall get my heart!"

"And I shall get my brains!" added the Scarecrow joyfully.

"And I shall get my courage!" the Lion agreed.

And I shall get the fuck out of here, I thought. As much as I was going to miss the sporadic nice parts, it was time. "We'll head out tomorrow morning."

We informed the Winkies of our plan to leave, and they seemed genuinely heartbroken. The following day, they presented each of us with a gift.

They gave Toto a golden collar, and me a bracelet studded with diamonds. They gave the Scarecrow a gold-headed walking stick, so he wouldn't fall over so much, which was pretty thoughtful. And they gave the Tin Woodsman a silver oil can, inlaid with gold and set with all different kinds of precious jewels. (They seemed *super* into the Tin Woodsman.)

They gave the Cowardly Lion a gold collar that looked just like Toto's but bigger, and by the look on his face I was afraid for a moment that he was going to bite one of them.

On the way out I swung by the kitchen to load up on snacks for the trip, and found the Witch's weird golden hat in one of the cupboards. I'm not above a little casual looting, so I stuffed it into my basket on a whim.

And with that, we were off.

CHAPTER XIV

THE WINGED MONKEYS.

The neighborhood surrounding the Witch's castle was *bleak as shit*. The sun rises in the east, though, so we kept it in front of us (and directly in our eyes, hooray), and plodded forward. Until about noon, when the sun had risen to its peak, and we had no idea where the hell we were going. We marched on as best we could—the Tin Woodsman had made this trip like two days before, but he was no help with directions at all—only to discover when the sun began sinking again that we had been travelling mostly south, and slightly back west, for at least an hour and a half. *Ugh.* We corrected course, but I wasn't sure if we should try to point a tiny bit northward to make up for lost time. The whole thing was a giant clusterfuck.

The next day was cloudy, and as much as we tried, we couldn't pinpoint the sun anywhere.

"Fuck it," I said. "We'll just walk, and if we don't find the Emerald City, at least we'll eventually run into something."

But the day passed away, and we didn't run into *shit*. "We have surely lost our way," the Scarecrow said mournfully. "And unless we find it again in time to reach the Emerald City, I shall never get my brains."

"Nor I my heart…" the Woodsman started.

"Jesus, can we *not* list all the things we're asking the Wizard for? Just this *once*?"

There was a brief pause. "I haven't the courage to keep tramping forever," the Cowardly Lion whispered, "without getting anywhere at all."

I plopped down onto the dirt and groaned. Toto sat beside me, and when a butterfly fluttered past his little head, he didn't have the energy to frolic around and chase it, even though that was pretty much his whole deal. Even though the day was overcast, it was somehow still blisteringly hot, so I tried in vain to fan myself with the Witch's gaudy-ass hat.

"If anybody has any ideas," I said. "I'm all ears."

"Perhaps we could call upon the mice," the Woodsman said.

"What *mice*?"

"The field mice, who helped us rescue the Lion from the poppy field. Their Queen said we could call upon them any time, and they would be happy to aid us."

"Okay," I said. "Sure. How do we call the field mice?"

"With this whistle the queen gave me." He pulled out a little whistle on a chain, and blew it, making an almost inaudible sound.

"When did she give you a *whistle*?" I decided that it didn't matter. Within minutes, we heard the pattering of tiny feet, and mice came running up from every direction. Apparently one of them was the Queen herself, although I still couldn't really tell them apart.

"What can I do for my friends?" she asked in her squeaky mouse voice.

"We need directions," I said. "We're trying to get back to the Emerald City."

"Certainly," answered the Queen, "but it is a great way off, and you have had it at your backs all this time." Which, of course, begged the question of how the mice were able to get to us so quickly. Had they been *following us*?

But then the Queen noticed the Witch's hat. "Why don't you use the charm of the Cap, and call the Winged Monkeys to you? They will carry you to the City of Oz in less than an hour."

"Wait, *what*?"

"The spell is written inside the golden cap," she said. "But if you are going to call the Winged Monkeys we must run away, for they are full of mischief and think it great fun to plague us."

The whole business reminded me of some stupid computer game. I didn't play them much (because, like I said, *stupid*), but Madeline liked them, so I occasionally got stuck watching *her* play. And I couldn't escape the feeling that the mouse whistle was the cheat function, where you got a hint when you couldn't figure out what to do next.

Was I overthinking the whole thing? Sure, desensitizing you to wanton violence and forcing you into situations where you had to murder was probably how the KGB brainwashed assassins. But it also described most video games, as far as I could tell. If all this was just some super-advanced virtual reality game (again, possibly enhanced with hallucinogens?), I'd be—

Well, I wasn't sure if I'd be relieved or pissed. But the idea did make me want to finally be done with it as soon as possible.

The Scarecrow and Woodsman were exchanging frightened glances and shaking their heads. "No Winged Monkeys," the Woodsman pleaded.

"Oh, do not worry," the Mouse Queen said. "They must obey the wearer of the Cap, and will not harm you. Goodbye!"

She scampered out of sight, with all the mice hurrying after her. I looked inside the Golden Cap, and sure enough, instructions were stitched in there, with some gibberish to speak and a small amount of hopping.

"Ep-pe, pep-pe, kak-ke," I said, standing on my left foot. I felt like an asshole.

"I don't know what that means," the Scarecrow said.

I ignored him, and continued the spell, shifting to my right foot. "Hil-lo, hol-lo, hel-lo."

"Hello!" The Woodsman waved back at me.

I hopped back onto both feet "Ziz-zy, zuz-zy, zik!" That was the end of it, and I immediately heard flapping wings, and the Flying Monkeys' trademark chattering. Moments later, the sky was riddled with them.

The Monkey King came in for a landing, and bowed at my feet, "What is your command?"

"Take us to the Emerald City," I said. "*Carefully*. And don't kill any of us this time."

"As you wish," he said. If he was at all bitter about being ordered around by a girl in a stupid hat, he certainly didn't show it. Another big monkey flew in, and the two of them picked me up gently and carried me into the sky. Others swooped down and lifted the Scarecrow, Woodsman and Lion. A smallish one picked up Toto, and damn near got himself bitten for his trouble.

Even by air, the trip wasn't short. Eventually I got bored with majestic vistas, and turned to the Monkey King.

"So what's the whole deal with the goofy hat?"

"That is a long story," he said. "But as we have a long journey before us, I will pass the time by telling you about it, if you wish."

Ugh. "Sure, why not."

"Once," he began, "we were a free people, living happily in the great forest, flying from tree to tree, eating nuts and fruit, and doing just as we pleased without calling anybody master."

The Monkey King wasn't kidding when he said that his story was long. But the gist of it was that there was a beautiful princess/powerful sorceress named Gayelette who everybody loved, but who couldn't find anyone to love in return because all the men were stupid and ugly, and she was probably a lesbian.

"At last, however," the Monkey King continued, "she found a boy who was handsome and manly and wise beyond his years. Gayelette made up her mind that when he grew to be a man she would make him her husband."

Ew. She took the kid back to her castle and basically raised him, and when he was eventually far enough past puberty, got ready to marry him. *Awesome*.

"My grandfather was at that time the King of the Winged Monkeys which lived in the forest near Gayelette's palace," the Monkey King said. "And the old fellow loved a joke better than a good dinner." So he picked up the Prince, or whatever he was, and dumped him in the river, which I guess seemed hilarious at the time. The Prince actually thought it was funny too, and was super chill about it, but Gayelette lost her shit, because the water *ruined his fancy clothes.*

At first I thought Gayelette sounded pretty cool, but clearly she was the worst. I remembered the Wicked Witch—powerful women in these old stories were *always* the worst. Imagine that. Anyway, Gayelette sentenced every single Flying Monkey to be tied up, dumped in the river and drowned. But the Prince talked her out of it, so instead they all agreed to grant three wishes to whoever owned the gold hat (it had been a wedding present or something) for all eternity.

Three wishes? "Hey, can you fly me all the way out of Oz, and back to my home in Calabasas?"

"That cannot be done," he said. "We belong to this country alone, and cannot leave it. There has never been a Winged Monkey in Calabasas yet, and I suppose there never will be, for they don't belong there." Well, it was worth a shot.

He finished his story. "The Prince was the first owner of the Golden Cap, and after he was married he ordered us always to fly far away and keep where the Princess could never again set eyes on a Winged Monkey. Which we were glad to do, for we were all afraid of her."

Fair enough. "This was all we ever had to do until the Golden Cap fell into the hands of the Wicked Witch of the West," he continued. "She made us enslave the Winkies, and afterward drive Oz himself out of the Land of the West. Now the Golden Cap is yours, and three times you have the right to lay your wishes upon us."

And with that, we had arrived at the Emerald City. The Monkeys set us down carefully at the gates, the King bowed low, and they flew away. I decided that, if things went as planned and we were close to the end of this thing, I'd do that thing where I used my last wish to free the Monkeys from having to grant any more wishes.

"That was a good ride," the Scarecrow said.

"Yes, and a quick way out of our troubles," the Lion agreed. "How lucky it was you brought away that wonderful cap!"

I mean, we *were* almost done, right? In the movie, this was the part where the Wizard gave us half-assed diplomas and watches and stuff, and then fucked off in a balloon while Glinda came and told me the secret shoe password, and I got the hell back to Kansas. If this *was* a video game, though, it really felt like I'd have to use the Golden Cap two more times. Which meant there could be a *whole bunch of stuff* left to do that wasn't in the film.

Fuuuuuuuuuuuuck.

THE DISCOVERY OF OZ, THE TERRIBLE.

W e rang the bell at the front gate, and were greeted by the same Guardian Dude from—what was it, a week ago? *Two* weeks? I couldn't even keep track.

"What! Are you back *again*?" he asked.

"Don't act so surprised."

"But I thought you had gone to visit the Wicked Witch of the West."

"We did visit her," the Scarecrow said.

"And she let you go again?"

"She could not help it, for she is melted," the Scarecrow explained.

"From a *bucket of water*," I added. "It was *not* that hard."

"Good gracious!" He bowed very low, then brought us into the room with the box full of gross, sweaty sunglasses to affix to our faces. I was pretty much done with that part, though.

"I am Dorothy the Witchkiller," I said. "I melted one, and crushed the other beneath a house. My eyes cannot be blinded by even the gaudiest interior design, so I'm all set, thanks."

I never did manage to convince the others that the whole thing was just a hoax, so they all took the green shades, and I let them put a pair on Toto, too, so they wouldn't sic Munchkin PETA on my ass or whatever.

Once we entered the city proper and were on our way to the Wizard's palace, I almost regretted my decision. Without the glasses, the place didn't look any greener than your average fairy tale metropolis, but all those glittering gems made it bright as *balls*.

News spread quickly of the witch melting, and by the time we reached the palace we were surrounded by a cheering crowd. So that was kind of rad. The soldier—whose beard was actually brown with flecks of gray, incidentally—went straight to alert the Wizard to our presence, while Concierge Girl brought us to our usual parlor to wait for him.

And wait we did. Two hours later, I was about ready to sneak out and find a bath somewhere to wash the Flying Monkey off me. Finally, the soldier popped his head into the room and whispered something into Concierge Girl's ear.

"Oz the Great and Terrible needs time to prepare for you," she said. "I will show you to your rooms, and he'll be ready to receive you in the morning." She winced. "Or perhaps the next day, or the day after that."

Like hell. If I'd wanted any more days of lounging around doing nothing, I would have done it back at Winkie Castle. And as eager as I was to bathe—

Actually, the faint whiff of monkey reminded me of something. Didn't the Monkey King say one of his jobs for the Wicked Witch was to shoo Oz off her land?

"You tell that Wizard that I command the Flying Monkeys," I said, "and if there's some reason he can't see us today, he can explain it to *them*."

That seemed to do the trick, because she disappeared, and moments later we were hurried into Oz's throne room. Inside, we didn't find a big floating head, a hot girl, a giant monster *or* a ball of fire. In fact, the place was empty.

Had the Wizard just taken off? After a minute, a voice came from a hidden speaker somewhere near the top of the domed room.

"I am Oz, the Great and Terrible! Why do you seek me?"

I looked around and didn't see a curtain anywhere. There was, however, a little screen set up in one corner. "You *know* why we seek you," I said. "Why don't you come out from your hiding place so we can get this over with?"

"I am not hiding!" he said. "I am everywhere! But to the eyes of common mortals I am invisible. I will now seat myself upon my throne, that you may converse with me." Sure enough, the last line sounded like it came from the throne. The Wizard was leaning on his hidden speaker trick *hard*.

Whatever. "We killed your witch, and we're back for our rewards."

"What rewards?" he demanded.

The Scarecrow seemed almost as tired of getting dicked around as I was. "You promised to give me brains!"

"And you promised to give me a heart!" the Woodsman said.

"And you promised to give me courage!" added the Lion.

"And you promised to send me home," I said. "We will also accept hollow platitudes and incompetent balloon piloting if it finally gets this *fucking* plot moving."

There was a pause. "Is the Wicked Witch really destroyed?" Now there was definitely a tremble in the voice.

"Yup," I said. "Melted with a bucket of water."

"Oh, man," said the Voice. "*Man!* Well, come to me tomorrow, for I must have time to think it over."

"You've had plenty of time already," the Tin Woodsman said angrily.

"We shan't wait a day longer!" the Scarecrow agreed.

The Lion chimed in with a fierce roar, which was so loud that Toto jumped away from him in alarm and tipped over the screen in the corner. Sure enough, behind it was a frumpy little man. He wasn't, like, *Wizard of Oz* old, but maybe thirty-five or forty, with a scruffy red beard all over his face and neck, like no one had ever taught him how to shave.

"I am Oz, the Great and Terrible," he said, his voice trembling even more now. "Please don't hit me."

"Okay," I said. "What the hell?"

"Hush, my dear," he said. I decided right then and there that if he called me "my dear" one more time, I *would* punch him. "Don't speak so loud," he continued, "or you will be overheard, and I should be ruined. I'm supposed to be a Great Wizard!"

"And aren't you?" the Scarecrow asked.

"Not a bit. I'm just a common man."

"You're more than that," I said. "You're a *fucking douchebag.*"

"Yeah, I guess I am," he said.

"But this is terrible!" said the Woodsman. "How shall I ever get my heart?"

"Or I my courage?" asked the Lion.

"Or I my brains?" wailed the Scarecrow, wiping the tears from his eyes with his coat sleeve.

"You think *you* have problems?" said Oz, "What about *me*? What about the terrible trouble I'm going to be in now that I've been found out?"

"You mean nobody else has figured out that you're a douchebag?" I asked.

"No one knows it but you four—and myself," he said. "I have fooled everyone so long that I thought I'd never be found out. I guess it was a mistake my ever letting you into the throne room. Usually I won't even see my subjects, and so they believe I'm something terrible."

He showed us a small chamber in the back of the throne room where he hid all of his tricks—the giant head was just paper mache, with obvious wires that worked the eyes and mouth. The one I saw back when we first arrived *definitely* had better special effects than this one did, but it's not like I was fooled anyway, so I didn't make a stink. He also showed us the mask and dress he had worn to appear as a beautiful woman to the Scarecrow, and when the Woodsman saw it, he actually shuddered. He clearly had a fair amount of fantasy time invested in the mysterious Lady, based solely on the Scarecrow's description.

"And the Beast was a statue, and the fireball was a bag of flaming trash, we get it," I said. "And you have speakers in the walls and chair to make your voice come from wherever."

"Oh, there are no speakers in Oz," he said. "I am a trained ventriloquist! I can throw the sound of my voice wherever I wish! Sit down, please, there are plenty of chairs. I will tell you my story."

"Ugh. Fine, but make it quick."

"I was born in the faraway land of Van Nuys, California—"

Van Nuys? "That's right by Studio City, where my Dad lives!"

"Wait. You're from the *real world*?" His face went white. "Oh my god. It's been so long."

He grabbed me by my hoodie. "Tell me the news! Did the Super Nintendo ever come out? Was Mode 7 as revolutionary as they said? And what of *Final Fantasy II*?"

He was shaking now. "Tell me, *what of Final Fantasy II*?"

If *Final Fantasy* was the video game I was thinking of, I was pretty sure they were up to like fifteen or twenty by now. This guy *had* been in Oz a long time. "It's so good," I said. "You should come back and play it with me. You'll love it."

He shook his head gravely. "I was just a kid," he said. "I went into a new shop in the Galleria, and they said they had the latest virtual reality technology, but when I went into the booth I blacked out, and woke up on a hot air balloon, floating over a strange and beautiful country."

His story sounded awfully familiar. "It came down gradually," he continued, "and I was not hurt a bit. But I found myself in the midst of a strange people, who, seeing me come from the clouds, thought I was a great Wizard. Of course I let them think I was, because they were afraid of me, and promised to do anything I wished. I ordered them to build this city, and my palace, and they did it all happily."

"And when we finally showed up, you didn't figure out that you were inside the plot of *The Wizard of Oz*?"

"I never watched *The Wizard of Oz*! My sister watched it a lot, so I knew a little something about it, but it always seemed like kind of a girl thing."

He explained that he had spent decades afraid of the evil Witches from the east and west, so when I came and killed one of them, he was willing to offer me whatever I wanted to take care of the other. "But, now that you have melted her," he said, "I'm ashamed to say that I can't keep my promises."

"Because you're a *douchebag*," I said.

"No!" he insisted. "I'm a really nice guy! But I'm a very bad Wizard, I must admit."

The Scarecrow was forlorn. "Can't you give me brains?"

"You don't need them! You're learning something every day. A baby has brains, but it doesn't know much. Experience is the only thing that brings knowledge, and the longer you are on earth the more experience you get."

"That may all be true," said the Scarecrow, "but I shall be very unhappy unless you give me brains."

The Wizard looked at him carefully and scratched his beard.

"Well," he said with a sigh, "I'm not much of a magician, but if you come to me tomorrow morning, I will stuff your head with brains. I cannot tell you how to use them, however. You must find that out for yourself."

The Scarecrow was over the moon. "Oh, thank you—thank you! I'll find a way to use them, never fear!"

"But how about my courage?" the Lion asked.

"You have plenty of courage, man," answered Oz. "All you need is confidence in yourself. There is no living thing that is not afraid when it faces danger. True courage is in facing danger when you are afraid, and that kind of courage you have in plenty."

"Perhaps. But can you give some of the other kind?"

"Very well, I will give you that sort of courage tomorrow," he said.

I was about ninety percent sure that by tomorrow we'd discover that the Wizard had skipped town.

"How about my heart?" the Tin Woodsman asked.

"Why, as for that," Oz said, "I think you are wrong to want a heart. It makes most people unhappy."

"That must be a matter of opinion," said the Woodsman. "For my part, I will bear all the unhappiness without a murmur, if you will give me the heart."

"Very well. Come to me tomorrow and you shall have a heart. I have played Wizard for so many years that I may as well continue the part a bit longer."

"Okay," I said. "So how are you going to get me home?"

"We shall have to think about that," he said. "Give me two or three days to consider the matter and I'll try to find a way to carry you over the desert."

"What about the balloon? Do you still have the balloon?"

"I said I need time to think! In the meantime you shall all be treated as my guests. There is only one thing I ask in return for my help, such as it is. You must keep my secret and tell no one I am a fake."

We agreed. I was fairly confident that the next part would follow the book, and he'd balloon off by himself and I'd have to somehow figure out how to use the shoes to get home. But I looked at my friends, whose faces were all filled with hope.

If he tried to ditch us without giving them each their magic feather or whatever, I was going to kick that little gremlin's ass.

CHAPTER XVI

THE MAGIC ART OF THE GREAT DOUCHEBAG.

We met at breakfast the following morning, and the Scarecrow was so excited he could hardly contain himself.

"Congratulate me," he said. "For I am going to Oz to get my brains at last. When I return I shall be as other men are!"

Oh, sweetheart, I thought, looking into his painted-on, dead eyes. *It's not your brains that are the problem.* "You're fine how you are," I insisted.

"It is kind of you to like a Scarecrow," he replied. "But surely you will think more of me when you hear the splendid thoughts my new brain is going to turn out."

The Wizard was trying to pull his schtick where he made us each come visit him alone, but at this point I didn't trust him enough for that. So when the soldier came to escort the Scarecrow to the throne room, I insisted that we all accompany him. Apparently my stock had risen around here since the most recent witch murder, because he didn't try to stop us.

"Come in," Oz said when the soldier rapped on his door.

We entered and found him sitting on his throne, feet dangling, seemingly engaged in deep thought.

"I have come for my brains," the Scarecrow said, a little uneasily.

"Oh, yes. Sit down in that chair, please," the Wizard said. "You must excuse me for removing your head, but I have to do it in order to put your new brains in their proper place."

"That's all right," said the Scarecrow. "You are quite welcome to take my head off, as long as it will be a better one when you put it on again."

So the Wizard untied the Scarecrow's head and emptied out the straw. The scarecrow's face continued to move and shift expressions on the folds of the empty head sack.

Aaaagh.

Then the Wizard went to his secret closet and came back with a big scoop of what looked like oat bran, mixed in with pins and needles. He dumped it into the Scarecrow's head, and filled up the rest of the space with straw.

"Hereafter you will be a great man," he said, "for I have given you a lot of bran-new brains."

Groan. The Scarecrow, however, was straight-up *delighted.*

"How do you feel?" I asked.

"I feel wise indeed," he answered earnestly. "When I get used to my brains I shall know everything!"

"Why are those needles and pins sticking out of your head?" the Woodsman asked.

"That is proof that he is sharp!" remarked the Lion.

"Well, I suppose I am next," the Woodsman said. He stepped nervously up to the Wizard. "I have come for my heart."

"Very well," Oz said. "But I shall have to cut a hole in your breast, so I can put your heart in the right place. I hope it won't hurt you."

What? "Do it through his back!" I said. The Winkie tinsmiths had spent *days* carefully reconstructing his sleek, shiny torso, and I was pretty sure this guy was going to cut right in and make a mess of him.

"Either way," the Woodsman said. "I shall not feel it at all."

So Oz picked up a pair of shears and cut a small, square hole in the Tin Woodsman's back. Then he went to a drawer and pulled out a stuffed, silk heart. It was actually sort of pretty.

"Isn't it a beauty?" he asked.

"It is, indeed!" the Woodsman said. "But is it a kind heart?"

"Oh, very," he insisted. He crammed the heart into the Woodsman's torso, and I thought I heard a muffled sound when it fell, possibly into one of his legs or something. Then the Wizard replaced the square of tin and picked up some kind of gas-powered soldering rig, sealing the hole back up.

When he was done, it actually didn't look too bad. "There," he said. "Now you have a heart that any man might be proud of. I'm sorry I had to put a patch on your back, but it really couldn't be helped."

"Never mind the patch," exclaimed the Woodsman. "I am very grateful to you, and shall never forget your kindness!"

Then the Tin Woodsman rejoined the group, holding back tears of joy. The Lion was up next, and approached the throne shaking. *Extra* cowardly.

"I have come for my courage," he said in a small voice.

"Very well," the Wizard said. "I will get it for you."

He went back to his closet and took a square bottle off the top shelf, which, unlike most of the stuff in the throne room, was actually green. Then he poured it into an intricately carved, ornate dish, and placed it at the Lion's feet. A potion to ease the Lion's anxiety? For all I knew, it really might be Klonopin. Or, you know, alcohol.

"Drink," the Wizard said.

The Lion sniffed at it, and made a face. "What is it?"

"Well," the Wizard said, "if it were inside of you, it would be courage. You know, of course, that courage is always inside one. So that this really cannot be called courage until you have swallowed it. Therefore I advise you to drink it as soon as possible."

So, *definitely* alcohol. The Wizard's speech was all the Lion needed to hear, though. He lapped up every last drop.

"How do you feel now?" asked Oz.

"*Full* of courage!" the Lion replied. He joined the Woodsman and

Scarecrow, and the three of them congratulated each other and hugged and patted one another on the back.

"But what of Dorothy?" the Scarecrow asked when they had settled down a bit. "How will you grant her wish?"

"Why don't you guys leave us alone for a few minutes while we figure that part out," I said. "Go show off your new organs and stuff to the castle guards. I won't be too long."

I turned to the Wizard once the door had closed. "That was actually very kind of you."

"No amount of trickery can make a wise man out of a fool," he said, "Although it's easy enough to make the fool believe he is wise. You know far better than I whether or not the lot of them have had smarts, and kindness, and bravery inside them all along."

"Trust me," I said. "They'll be fine. Now, let's talk about how you're going to get me back to sunny California."

"I thought a great deal about your balloon suggestion," he said. His old-timey speech patterns seemed to come and go—when we'd surprised him the day before he had mostly reverted to normal-person speech, but today he was talking all fancified again.

"The contraption I arrived in was destroyed long ago, but I think I may be able to construct a new one. It's high time you were returned to your home, young lady."

Hell yeah, it was.

"And high time for me, as well. For I shall be coming with you!"

HOW THE BALLOON
WAS LAUNCHED.

was okay with that. I had actually been pretty much expecting it. But something about the way he said it got under my skin. Also, I was trying not to think too much about the implications of running into another visitor from the real world in that place. Of course, it could be that whatever video game thing I was in was just multiplayer, and he was bullshitting me about having been stuck there for decades. Or it could be that I... *had actually been transported to the magical land of Oz?*

Whatever. I was almost out of there anyway.

The following day, I heard nothing from Oz. My friends all seemed happy and content—the Scarecrow insisted that he was having all kinds of amazing, secret thoughts in his head, and the Lion declared that he now feared nothing, and would gladly fight a hundred Kalidahs. The Woodsman, of course, discovered his new heart to be far kinder and more tender than the flesh one he used to have. They were all a little quiet and nervous around me, though—partly, I think, because they didn't want to make too big a deal about their rad gifts when they knew I hadn't received mine yet, and partly because they didn't want to see me go.

Finally, just after dinner, Oz sent the beardy soldier to fetch me and escort me to the throne room. The Wizard was sitting on his throne, with huge sheets of green silk in every shade piled up all around him.

I narrowed my eyes. "That's *not* a balloon."

"The balloon," he said, "will be made of silk, and coated with glue to keep the gas in. I have gathered up all the finest materials in the palace! Now all we have left to do is construct it."

"What do you mean *we*? You have like a million people at your command. Order *them* to make the balloon."

"But surely you see I cannot!" I was starting to figure out his pattern. The more full of shit he was, the more he spoke all old-timey like the rest of the people in Oz. But when I had him flustered, he reverted to his natural speech.

For now, he was in full bluster. "The wondrous flying contraption was the very thing that convinced the people I was a wizard to begin with. If any of them discover it's something they can *make themselves*, I'll be found out!"

"So? You're leaving anyway. Why do you even care?"

"I have my legacy to think of! Also, what if the contraption *fails*? Though I'm quite certain of my design, it *is* the first balloon I've ever technically constructed."

Ugh. "Fine, what do I need to do?"

"I shall cut strips of silk into their proper shape, and you shall sew them neatly together."

"Fuck that," I said. "I'll cut and you sew."

"But I've never stitched anything in my life. I'd surely make a mess of it."

"Neither have I! What, you think women just sit around and have *sewing circles*? Come on. I know you're from the 1980s, at *least*."

"We're only wasting our time by arguing about it," Oz said. "It will take us three whole days to finish the task as it is."

What? "The hell it will. Let me get my friends in to help. They already know you're full of shit."

"I'm afraid they'll be no use. The Tin Woodman's mechanical fingers were not built for such a delicate task, and the Scarecrow's stuffed mitts couldn't even hold a needle. As for the Cowardly Lion, an animal such as he *certainly* lacks the manual dexterity."

Manual dexterity? That gave me an idea. It might not be the wisest use of my two remaining wishes, but I'd be damned if I was going to spend the following three days sewing.

I pulled the golden cap out of my basket and stood on one foot. "Ep-pe, pep-pe, kak-ke."

"What is this?" Oz looked befuddled. "Are you throwing a *fit*?"

"Hil-lo, hol-lo, hel-lo." I finished my hopping. "Ziz-zy, zuz-zy, zik." There was a low, rumbling sound, and the entire throne room shook. Then, with a crash, dozens of Flying Monkeys burst through the chamber doors.

Oz screamed and scrambled behind his screen, stumbling on the way and half-sliding across the throne room floor.

"You're not welcome here!" he howled. It sounded like he was trying to do his booming Wizard voice, but it just came out like a desperate yelp. "Begone! Go back to your... wherever you go!"

The Monkey King landed on the floor and bowed. "This is the second time you have called us," he said. "What do you wish?"

"Build this balloon for me," I said. "The silk needs to be cut into the shape of that pattern over there, and then all stitched together into, like, a balloon shape. *Super* delicately."

"As you wish." They got to work, and with their little opposable monkey thumbs, turned out to be magnificent seamstresses. Between the whole troop of them, they finished the job inside of forty-five minutes. The result- ing balloon was massive, more than twenty feet from top to bottom. I had them spread it out to show the Wizard, who hadn't come out from behind his screen the entire time.

"How's it look?" I asked. "Are we done?"

He risked a tiny peek. "We still have to put the glue in there," he said. "I haven't had a chance to mix it up yet! I thought it... *I thought we had like three days!*"

"Well, get to it," I said. He slowly made his way across the room to his secret closet, keeping his back against the wall. Meanwhile, the Flying Monkeys were getting restless without a task to keep them busy. They started chattering and fluttering around, picking emeralds out of the walls and peeling the upholstery off the throne. By the time the Wizard finished cooking his adhesive, they had pretty much trashed the place.

I was okay with that.

I ordered them to spread a thin coating inside the balloon, then hang it up on the domed ceiling to dry. I had to admit, it looked magnificent, with alternating patterns of silk, and flawless workmanship. The Wizard begrudgingly agreed, and deemed the craft skyworthy.

With another bow, the Monkey King spread his wings and flew out through the window, followed by each of his subjects in turn.

"Okay, are we set?" I asked. "Is it ready to fly?"

"It will need to sit overnight for the glue to dry," the Wizard said. "And we'll need a basket. I think the great baskets they use in the laundry room will do nicely."

Of course he made his servants cart his dirty clothes around in baskets *big enough to ride in.*

"And then there's the matter of filling it with gas, for there is no hydrogen or helium in the kingdom of Oz."

"So, what do we use? Fairy dust? Kalidah farts?"

"Oh, there is another, quite natural way to make it float, which is to fill it with hot air. It's simple physics! When air is heated it becomes lighter than the cool air around it, and shall cause the balloon to rise." With the monkeys gone, he was becoming his old, pompous self again.

"Whatever, dude." I left him to his pontificating and went to check in with my friends, then settle in for what would hopefully, FOR THE LOVE OF MOTHERFUCKING GOD, finally be my last night in Oz.

The next morning, what looked like the entire city had gathered to watch the launch. The Wizard was already in the basket when I arrived. He had attached big, canvas fins to the sides of the balloon, connected with pulleys, apparently to give him the ability to steer it. The whole thing was strapped down to a wooden platform by a few thin ropes that seemed woefully inadequate for the task.

Oz was addressing the crowd. "Today I leave to visit my great brother Wizard who lives in the clouds," he pronounced, to thunderous applause. "While I am gone the Scarecrow will rule over you. I command you to obey him as you would me!"

The citizenry was eating it up with a spoon. "Come, Dorothy!" Oz said. "Hurry, or the balloon will fly away!"

The thing was, I wasn't sure if I wanted to. In the movie, the balloon accidentally launched without Dorothy, and she had to use her slippers to get home. But the magic slippers were the first thing I tried, back when this whole thing started. Could it be I was *supposed* to take the balloon in this version? Should I just make the goodbye speeches now, and get on with it? The Scarecrow, Tin Woodsman, and Lion were at my side, all looking terribly forlorn.

"Wait!" the Scarecrow said. "Where is Toto?"

Chasing a cat, if I remembered correctly? "He's actually the least of my worries right now."

The Wizard had his arms out, beckoning me to come aboard. "But you can't leave your dog behind," he said. "You must take him home with you!"

Must? "He loves it here. He'll be fine. Or do you mean I have to take him to finish the story? Like it's some sort of *victory condition*?"

The ropes creaked, and the balloon made a small lurch toward the sky. Now the Wizard was starting to panic. "I don't know the *rules*! Forget the dog! The ropes are breaking!"

"Wait!" None of this felt right. "I don't know if I'm *supposed* to go."

"You have to!" Now he was utterly freaking out. "I've been trapped here for so long—I need to find out *why*! I can't do it by myself! I never would have even gotten the idea for this stupid balloon if you hadn't brought it up!"

There was a loud crack as the cables snapped, and the balloon careened into the air. "No!" Oz shouted. "I can't bring it back down until the hot air cools on its own!" In mere moments, the balloon disappeared into the clouds, and the Wizard's cries disappeared along with it.

Which was fine, right? He goes up in the balloon, I get all upset and pout for a minute, then the Good Witch of the North shows up to teach me how to work my shoes, and *boom*, it's happily ever after. The Scarecrow, Woodsman and Lion were doing their part, orating mournfully about the injustice of it all. The assembled cityfolk were also quite upset, having realized that their Wizard was, in all likelihood, never coming back. I just closed my eyes and stood there, waiting for the Witch.

The Good Witch of the North never came.

AWAY TO THE SOUTH.

"**F**uck. Fuck fuck fuck fuck *fuck*."

That was pretty much all I had managed to get out in the entirety of the three hours we'd spent convening in the Wizard's throne room, trying to figure out what to do next.

"Don't fret, Dorothy," the Scarecrow said earnestly. "If we all put our heads together I'm sure we'll come up with something yet." I looked deep into his painted-on, burlap eyes.

"FUUUUUUUUUUUUUUUUUUUUUUUUCK."

I'd screwed up. The Wizard had said he *never would have thought of the balloon if I hadn't mentioned it*. What if he was right? What if there was no balloon in the original Oz book, and I had accidentally given him that idea instead of whatever he was supposed to do? *Oh, shit*. I had used up a Flying Monkey wish building the thing, too. If the *real* ending required two more of those, I was *doublefucked*.

Should I throw on the hat and make the monkeys go grab the Wizard and haul him back to Earth? Where would that even *get* me? I was sure Oz would just try to get me into that fucking balloon again. If I went with him, and it *was* the wrong idea, what were the chances we'd both wind up dead somewhere in the desert? And even if the Wizard *did* have a backup plan, it would probably hinge on Flying Monkeys, and I'd have used up my last wish. No, that guy was basically useless. I was better off keeping the monkeys in my back pocket.

"We are not *so* unlucky," the Scarecrow said. He was sitting on the throne—all of the Wizard's former subjects seemed perfectly content to have him as their new king, and if they weren't going to complain about it, I certainly wasn't. "When I remember that a short time ago I was up on a pole in a farmer's cornfield, and that now I am the ruler of this beautiful city, I am quite satisfied with my lot."

"I also am well-pleased with my new heart," the Tin Woodsman said. "And, really, that was the only thing I wished in all the world."

"For my part, I am content in knowing I am as brave as any beast that ever lived, if not braver," the Lion said modestly.

"Is there no chance that you might come to love the Emerald City as we do," the Scarecrow asked, "and that we might all be happy here together?"

I sighed. "It's not that I don't love you guys. The three of you—and the meat pies, of course—are the only part of this whole thing that's been tolerable. But I need to get home. Like, for real."

"Well, then, we all must help you do it," the Woodsman said, "but what can be done?"

We had already tried whistling for the Mouse Queen, but if she was some sort of a cheat code, she was a shitty one. She had zero ideas.

"What of this Glinda you mentioned?" the Lion asked. "The Good Witch of the North. Might she yet help us?"

"Oh, Glinda isn't the Good Witch of the North." The bearded soldier had been tidying up the throne room—he was thrilled that after twenty-five years loyal service, the new king had finally let him come inside. Now he took a break from sweeping up fallen gemstones and monkey feathers, and leaned on his broom. "The Good Witch of the North is Locasta Tattypoo."

"Are you sure? She gave me a Witch Kiss a couple of weeks ago, and I kept expecting her to show up again, but she never did."

"Kindly old woman?" the soldier asked. "Small like a Munchkin, with a jolly smile?"

"Um, yeah. That sounds like her."

"That's Locasta. I know her well, for she was always nice to me whenever she paid the Great Wizard a visit. Glinda is the Witch of the *South*. She is the most powerful of all the Witches, and rules over the Quadlings."

The Scarecrow's terrifying nightmare face lit up. "Do you think this Glinda would help Dorothy find a way home?"

"She might. Her castle stands on the edge of the desert, so she may know a way to cross it."

"And is she a Good Witch?" the Lion asked. "Not that I would be afraid to run across another Bad one, of course."

"The Quadlings think she is good. And she is kind to everyone. I have heard that Glinda is a beautiful woman, who knows how to keep young in spite of the many years she has lived."

"*Really*," the Tin Woodsman said, intrigued.

Jesus Christ. "Okay," I said. "How do I get there?"

"The way is straight to the south," he answered, "but it is said to be full of dangers to travelers. There are wild beasts in the woods, and a race of odd men who do not like strangers to cross their country."

"You still have the Golden Cap!" the Scarecrow said. "You can call upon the Flying Monkeys once more, and be in Glinda's kingdom at once!"

I thought it over, and as much as I dreaded the prospect of another walking tour, I just couldn't risk it. I was already one monkey command short, and I couldn't afford to squander the last one if there was any other way forward. Also, there was the whole thing about setting them free with my last wish. Could I really look the Monkey King in the eyes and say 'Sorry about eternal servitude, dude, but I didn't feel like walking?'

"I think I'm going to have to make this trip the hard way, guys."

"Then I shall go with you," the Lion declared. "I am tired of your city and long for the woods and the country again. I am really a wild beast, you know. Besides, you will need someone to protect you."

"That is true," agreed the Woodsman. "My axe may be of service, so I also will go with you to the Land of the South."

"When shall we start?" the Scarecrow asked.

"My liege!" the soldier exclaimed. "You've only just come to rule the Emerald City. Surely we can't spare you so soon!"

"If it wasn't for Dorothy I should never have had the brains that make me fit to rule," he said. "She lifted me from the pole in the cornfield and brought me to the Emerald City to begin with. So my good luck is all due to her, and I shall never leave her until she starts back to Kansas for good."

It hadn't actually occurred to me that, if we were running off script, the others might have better things to do than go traipsing across the countryside with me. But I was certainly happy to have them along. "Alrighty. Let's do this."

"We shall go tomorrow morning," the Scarecrow said. "Let us all get ready, for it will be a long, *long* journey."

Fuuuuuuuuuuuuuuuuuuuuuuuuuuuuuuck.

CHAPTER XIX

ATTACKED BY THE FIGHTING TREES.

The next morning, Concierge Girl brought my freshly-laundered clothes, then just stood kind of awkwardly by the door. It would be my last night in the Emerald City—was I expected to *tip* her? Did they even *have* money in Oz? She was kind of sticking one cheek out a little, like she was expecting a *kiss* or something?

I gave her a meat pie. She looked at it like it was a dead rat, then thanked me profusely and left.

We swung by the front gates to drop off the sunglasses that my companions still had bolted over their eyes, and this time the Guardian seemed absolutely heartbroken to see us go.

"You are now our ruler," he said to the Scarecrow. "You must come back to us as soon as possible!"

"I certainly shall if I am able," the Scarecrow replied. "But I must help Dorothy to get home, first."

It was all very charming, but the truth was, I had other things weighing on my mind. We headed due south—there was technically a road going in our general direction, but the countryside was pleasant enough, and by now we had gotten used to off-roading it. The sun was shining, the air was so fresh you could almost taste it, and Toto ran around us in circles, chasing moths and butterflies, barking merrily all the time.

I had settled into a bit of a funk.

After a few minutes we turned to take a last look at the Emerald City, a mass of towers and steeples and that big-ass dome of the Wizard's palace rising up above the city walls. At least it all looked green from the outside.

"Oz was not such a bad Wizard, after all," the Woodsman said, tapping his tin chest.

"He knew how to give me brains, and very good brains, too," the Scarecrow said.

"If Oz had taken a dose of the same courage he gave me," the Lion added, "he would have been a brave man."

I left it alone. As far as I was concerned, that guy was a fucking *dick*. He had been dropped into this land just like I had, but instead of spending any effort to get home, or even treating the people he met with basic human decency, he *pretended to be a god*, made them build a city for him, and then hid in his throne room for *literally decades* so they wouldn't find out he was a fraud. Fuck that guy.

If I was being honest, though, it wasn't the futhermucking Wizard that was bothering me. I'd had a restless night, and while I'd lain awake staring at hideous, ornate wainscoting, I was pretty sure I'd figured out what was really going on. I had made it to the end of the story, but the story hadn't ended. And it wasn't because I was playing a video game and I hadn't done the puzzles right. When that happens in a game, you just lose, and either quit or start over. You're not *trapped there forever*. No one would *ever* design a game like that.

No, the reason my stay in Oz hadn't ended after I'd killed the Wicked Witch was because in the real world I was laying in a hospital bed somewhere, and *my head wound was too severe to recover from the coma*.

It made more sense than any of my other theories. There was *no way* virtual reality technology had advanced enough that it encompassed all five of your senses and was utterly indistinguishable from the real world. And KGB brainwashing? *Come on.* At first I had discounted the idea that I was in a dream, because I'm pretty sure that, if anything, my subconscious would have gone with the Judy Garland version. But if I was stuck in a coma, you know what my loved ones would probably do while they waited tearfully by my side, hoping against hope that I'd recover?

Fucking *read to me.*

And although L. Frank Baum wasn't the sort of thing my Mom would choose, it was *totally* up Madeline's alley. She had received an off-brand Kindle knockoff for her birthday one year, and stuffed it full of free public domain shit. Plus, she was always trying to get me to read more. And my Mom would think it was all heartwarming and adorable, too—my Mom *loved* Madeline—so she'd just sit there and let her read whatever. My broken head was constructing a reality from this continuous audio input, but when it got to the part where it was supposed to wake up, it couldn't. And it might *never* be able to. The plot was over, but the story just *kept going.*

We walked all day, through gorgeous, boring farmland, and *nothing fucking happened.*

That night, asleep on the soft, long grass with nothing but the stars over me, I dreamed. I dreamed that I was back at the mall, browsing through shitty band t-shirts at Spencer's with Glinda the Good Witch from the movie and Madeline, who had such a big crush on Glinda that she could barely speak. But I *knew* it was a dream.

So I tried a trick I had been using to wake up from nightmares ever since I was a little girl. I had always loved my occasional flying dreams, and every once in a while I had a scary falling one. But at some point I picked up on the fact that in my dreams I never actually *landed.* I climbed up on a mall bench and jumped off. Sure enough, before I hit tile, I found myself awake, lying in a field with the Scarecrow staring down at me creepily, as per usual.

My sudden waking must have startled him. "Dorothy? Are you feeling well?"

"Shut up. I need to try something." The Lion was snoring away on his belly beside me, so I carefully climbed up on his back, planted my bare feet in his mane, and jumped.

I hit the ground hard, scraping the bottom of my foot on a rock. *Stupid.* If I was trapped in a coma, *of course* I wouldn't be able to just snap myself out of it willingly.

The thing was, once I *knew* I was in a dream, I could usually control what happened in it. But this… it definitely wasn't the real world, but it didn't exactly follow dream logic, either. Were the rules *different* for coma dreams? Compared to the hazy mall scene I had just woken from—the details of which were already dissipating in my head like cotton candy—this felt *utterly* real. My foot was throbbing at that very moment, and after I rubbed it to inspect the damage, and lifted my fingers to my lips, I could *taste the blood.*

It was completely unlike any dream I'd ever had, coma or otherwise. I mean, if Oz wasn't a real place, it was certainly indistinguishable from one. And as much as I had idly speculated about hallucinogenic drugs, people who were actually tripping could *tell* that their senses were wacked out. This wasn't like that at all.

There was a word for people who weren't able to distinguish between fantasy and reality. But I wasn't ready to start exploring *that* theory yet.

Needless to say, I didn't sleep much for the rest of the night. When morning came, I poked a little at my breakfast, and we resumed our journey south. My friends could see that something was wrong, but I laughed off their inquiries and claimed that I was only tired. Still, ever since we had left the Emerald City, I had been distant, and I'm sure they felt it acutely. My Mom always said I should go into construction, I was so good at putting up—

Walls? We crested a small hill and found ourselves staring at an impenetrably thick forest, cutting across the fields like a sheer cliff, extending to the east and west as far as the eye could see. *Oh, shit.* It was like my subconscious mind felt threatened by all my random questioning and introspection, and was shoving literal barriers up through cracks I had bored into my psyche.

"What shall we do now?" the Lion asked.

"The Flying Monkeys could carry us over these woods quite easily," the

Woodsman said.

"No Flying Monkeys," I said. "Not yet." I hadn't walked for a goddamned day and a half so that I could waste my last monkey wish on a *forest*. We walked through forests *all the time*. Besides, if it was my stupid brain making these woods, I should be able to make a pathway through it, right?

I closed my eyes and concentrated. *Make a pathway, make a pathway, make a pathway.*

"Hey," the Scarecrow called out. "I found a pathway!"

Crap. I had kind of been hoping that *wouldn't* work.

"There's a big tree with such wide-spreading branches that there's room to pass beneath," he said. "Right here! Follow me and I'll—AAAAAAAAAAAAAH!"

Just as he came under the first branches, they reached down, twisted around his limbs, picked him up and flung him over our heads into the field behind us. The Scarecrow wasn't injured, of course, but did have a bit of the stuffing knocked out of him.

Oh, that's how you want to play this, subconscious?

"There's another space between the trees over here," the Lion said.

"Let me try again," the Scarecrow said. "Perhaps this time I'll—AAAAAAAAAAAAH!" The branches immediately seized him and tossed him back out again.

The Scarecrow picked himself up and smoothed out a few lumps. "Surely a third attempt won't—"

"Whoa, whoa, whoa," I said. "Let's try a different strategy." I stepped up to the treeline, just out of the reach of any wooden limbs.

"Trees?" I shouted into the forest (and, you know, *whatever else* needed shouting into). "*Trees* are your big play here? We LITERALLY brought a TREE-CUTTING MACHINE. Woodsman! How many trees have you chopped down since I've met you?"

The Tin Woodsman planted his feet beside me and put his hands on his hips. "One hundred and seven," he said.

"One hundred and—wait, *what*?" I was going to say, like, *six*. Was the guy chopping trees down all night, every night, just out of *spite*? Well, whatever. "What I'm trying to say is, DO NOT FUCK with this guy."

The Woodsman lifted his axe and approached the treeline slowly, and when a big branch grabbed at him, he cut it in two with a single swing. The entire tree shook, as if in pain.

"Come on!" he shouted. "Be quick!" We rushed under the tree without a scratch, except for Toto, who yelped as he was caught by a small branch. But the Woodsman quickly put his axe through it and set the little dog free.

After that, the trees left us alone. Either it was just the outer row that was enchanted to keep out intruders, or we had scared this forest *shitless*. Either way, we were able to travel through the woods without trouble. It was dark in there, and the foliage looked ugly and twisted.

Subtle. If the symbolism of bringing my friends through the barriers of my subconscious mind was supposed to bring us closer together, though, it wasn't working. If anything, I was feeling even more alone. Because if all of this was a figment of my imagination, that included the three of them. How do you have a heart-to-heart with someone you *suspect you may have made up*? Like, if the Scarecrow asked me if something was wrong, was that just part of my brain trying to psychoanalyze? Or was he the part of me that knew I *hated* people asking me if something was wrong, throwing up a red flag?

Or was he the coma, *trying to distract me from the fact that I was in a fucking coma*?

I was starting to freak myself out. I have no idea how long we walked—it could have been minutes or hours. I was completely lost in my thoughts, few of which made logical sense. Was I *supposed* to bring the others with me into this forest? Should I be here *alone*? Should I be here *at all*?

Suddenly we came to the edge of the woods, only to find a high, white wall as bright and smooth as porcelain. Again, it stretched as far as the eye could see.

"I cannot think why this wall is here," the Scarecrow said, befuddled. "Nor what country it conceals."

I just stared at it, my eyes wide. "The wall is my sanity," I said. "Beyond it lies *madness*."

THE DAINTY CHINA COUNTRY.

The Tin Woodsman suggested that we have the Flying Monkeys carry us over the wall, but I shot him a dirty look, so he started chopping up branches to make a ladder. Were the trees he cut them from *sentient* trees? Did it even *matter* at this point? EVERYTHING in this fucking place moved and talked and had feelings. I mean, what was the *Lion* killing for his dinner every night? What were my *meat pies* made out of?

Aaaaaaaaaaaaagh.

"Rest your brains and do not worry about the wall," the Woodsman said. "When we have climbed over it, we shall know what is on the other side."

I assumed that the other side would just be a featureless void, or possibly a starry expanse with *Twilight Zone* clocks and shit floating around in it. Oz wasn't some fever dream. The whole hit-your-head-and-imagine-a-fantastic-adventure thing was a stupid television trope. And I hadn't passed out in some shitty mall store during an earthquake. *There never was a mall store.* I was now convinced that the real me was locked up in an institution somewhere, drooling onto a padded floor.

The real me was *out of her goddamned mind.*

When the Woodsman's ladder was finished, it looked in all honesty like a rickety piece of crap. He assured me that it was sturdy, though. There was nothing left to do but climb it.

So we did. And what wound up being on the other side of the big, porcelain wall was a whole porcelain town, with houses and buildings that barely reached past my knees. And little porcelain princes and princesses and shepherds and milkmaids and livestock and what have you. There was a terrifying porcelain clown.

Huh. They were all walking around and having conversations and stuff, because *of course they were.* None of them seemed to notice the assorted flesh, tin and straw giants who had appeared at the top of their wall, except for a porcelain dog with an oversized head, who made a tiny bark and then ran away.

The ladder was too heavy to pull up after us, so we tossed the Scarecrow down first and used him to break our fall. Even so, landing on the porcelain floor made the pain in my foot flare up again. If Oz *was* just a product of my insanity, recognizing it didn't seem to make anything hurt less.

We continued south, and the first thing we came across was a porcelain milkmaid milking a porcelain cow. It reminded of an actual porcelain horse that my Mom kept over the fireplace at home. Some old person from work had given it to her (old people *always* had whole shelves full of porcelain crap). Anyway, my Mom insisted that she only liked the horse *ironically.*

When the cow looked up and saw us, it suddenly gave a moo and kicked over the stool, the pail, and even the milkmaid herself. They all fell on the ground with a clatter.

"See what you have done!" the milkmaid cried. She sounded more angry than afraid. "My cow has broken her leg, and I must take her to the mender's shop and have it glued on again. What do you mean by coming here and frightening my cow?"

Sure enough, one of the cow's legs had broken clean off. "Um, sorry," I said.

She was too pissed off to even answer. She picked up the leg and led her cow away, the poor animal limping on three legs. She kept glancing over her shoulder and giving us the stink eye as she walked.

"We must be very careful here," said the Woodsman, "or we may hurt these pretty little people so they will never get over it."

A bit farther on, we came across a porcelain princess in a fancy dress. As soon as she spotted us, she bolted.

"Don't chase me! Don't chase me!" she screamed.

"Relax! We're not going to chase you!"

She finally stopped once she decided she was a safe distance away. "You see, if I run I may fall down and break myself."

"So don't run," I said. "And isn't there some kind of mender person? Can't you just go get fixed up?"

"Oh, yes," the princess said. "But one is never so pretty after being mended, you know," replied the princess.

Fair enough.

"See, there is Mr. Joker, one of our clowns," she continued. "He is always trying to stand upon his head. He has broken himself so often that he is mended in a hundred places, and doesn't look at all pretty."

The clown was the fucking *worst*. He was cracked all over, sure, but he also pranced around with big, exaggerated mime gestures, and kept trying to talk to us in rhyme.

"Don't mind Mr. Joker," the princess said. "He is considerably cracked in his head, and that makes him foolish."

I didn't actually care that much if the clown was an asshole. I just wanted to know if any of this was *real*. I got down on my knees to inspect the pint-sized princess up close. She certainly *looked* real. I stopped short of touching her, though. "What do you think? Do you want to come back to Calabasas with me and live above a fireplace with a porcelain horse?"

"That would make me very unhappy," she said. "You see, here in our country we live contentedly, and can talk and move around as we please.

But whenever any of us are taken away our joints at once stiffen, and we can only stand straight and look pretty. Of course that is all that is expected of us when we are on mantels and cabinets and drawing-room tables, but our lives are much pleasanter here in our own country."

Again with the sentient-mannequin-trapped-forever schtick—it was like a *theme* in this thing. Did that actually lend credence to the coma theory? Like, *I* was the paralyzed one, and my mind was trapped? I might have been overthinking it. We kept walking cautiously over porcelain farmland, and after an hour or so, came to another wall.

Was that *it*? Okay, that *had* to be me going crazy, right? Who would put that scene in a *book*? Nothing happened in it. What would the point even be? "Don't be mean to old people, because… *their knick-knacks are alive?*" Or DO be mean to them, because they're *fucking monsters who lure sentient porcelain creatures to their doom*?

The second wall wasn't as high as the first, and we were able to get over it by climbing on the Lion's back. Once we were on top of it, the Lion gathered his legs under him to jump over, but accidentally swiped a little porcelain church with his tail and smashed it to pieces.

Still, we had managed to get through the whole, fragile town and only broke one church and a cow leg, which I thought was pretty good. Also, I still seemed to be, like, *a person*, and my friends were still with me, which was comforting. So I hadn't completely descended into madness and despair yet.

That had to be a good sign.

THE LION BECOMES
THE KING OF BEASTS.

O n the other side of the wall, the terrain was boggy and marshy, and smelled like ass. It was difficult to get through without stepping into muddy holes, but we persevered. Eventually we came to solid ground, and walked through the underbrush into *another fucking forest*.

The trees here were taller and older than any we'd seen yet. "This forest is perfectly delightful," declared the Lion. "Never have I seen a more beautiful place."

"It seems gloomy to me," the Scarecrow said.

"Not a bit," the Lion answered. "I should like to live here all my life. See how soft the dried leaves are under your feet, and how rich and green the moss is that clings to these old trees? Surely no wild beast could wish a pleasanter home."

If that were true, no one had told the other wild beasts about it. We didn't encounter a single one for the rest of the day. When it became too dark to go any farther, Toto and I snuggled up against the Lion's hide to sleep, with the Woodsman and Scarecrow keeping watch as usual.

I was exhausted. At least the day's long trek had pushed some of the dark thoughts out of my mind. I had really started to lose my shit back in forest number one that morning, but the whole thing with the porcelain village was so weird and dumb that it actually kind of shook me out of my funk. And the more I thought about it, the more I decided that if Coma Patient Theater was a shitty trope, Mentally Ill Person Who Has Magical Adventures in Her Mind was an even shittier one. Schizophrenia was a very real, very tragic condition that a lot of people struggled with, but I was pretty sure it didn't manifest itself as a *Wizard of Oz* fantasy that looked and sounded and smelled like you were actually living it.

Which left me... well, I wasn't sure *where* it left me. But my feet were sore, I had kind of a dull ache all over my body, and my current plan was to fall asleep cuddling this lion and worry about it in the morning.

When morning came, I still had nothing. So we kept walking south. We'd eventually have to get to Glinda the Good Witch, or at least *something*. Right? Before long we heard a low rumbling of growling and snorting, and we discovered what had happened to all the animals in this forest.

They had all assembled for a *big ancient forest animal meeting*. There were tigers and elephants and bears and wolves and foxes and all kinds of stuff, some of which belonged in a forest and some of which didn't. They were all sort of snarling at each other—I guess when animals spoke among themselves they didn't bother with English?

Several of the beasts caught sight of the Cowardly Lion, and at once the great assemblage hushed as if by magic. The biggest of the tigers came up to the Lion and bowed.

"Welcome, o King of Beasts," he said. "You have come in good time to fight our enemy and bring peace to all the animals of the forest once more."

Okay, this should be good. "What is your trouble?" the Lion asked. His tone was *statesmanlike*.

"We are all threatened by a fierce enemy which has lately come into this forest," the tiger said. "It is a most tremendous monster, like a great spider, with a body as big as an elephant and eight legs as long as a tree trunk. As the monster crawls through the forest he seizes an animal with one of his legs and drags it to his mouth, where he eats it as a spider does a fly. Not one of us is safe while this fierce creature is alive, and we had called a meeting to decide how to take care of ourselves when you came among us."

The Tin Woodsman's face lit up. "The Flying Monkeys!" he said. "Surely an army of them could conquer this horrible beast."

Here was the thing about the Flying Monkeys. I had told myself that I would need my last wish to win some video game I was playing, and as long as I hung onto it, some tiny part of me could *still believe that was true.* Or, even if I was trapped here by a head injury or undiagnosed psychosis or whatever, playing by the rules I had imposed upon myself meant that I was *trying* to get through it, the only way I knew how. Using up my last *deus ex monkeyna* would feel like I was giving up, and somehow *surrendering to Oz.*

Fortunately, the Lion saved me from having to make that decision. "No," he said. "This is *my* battle." He addressed the tiger. "If I put an end to your enemy, will you bow down to me and obey me as King of the Forest?"

"We will do that gladly," the tiger said. And all the other beasts roared mightily:

"We will!"

"Where is this great spider of yours now?"

"Yonder, among the oak trees," the tiger said, pointing with his paw.

"Take good care of these friends of mine," the Lion said, "and I will go at once to fight the monster."

"Hold up," I said. "I'm coming with."

The Lion protested, whispering to me that if he didn't go alone, the other animals might not accept him as their lord and ruler. But I convinced him that they couldn't possibly dock him points for bringing along a ten-year-old girl. If anything, it was *more* impressive that he could dispatch a horrible beast while having to worry about keeping me safe while he did it. The fact was, I was desperate to find some whiff of plot that would give me the slightest hope that I was still voyaging through literature, and I could just get to the end of the book and go home. It was a long shot, sure, but the giant spider was the closest thing to actual story structure we'd come across since leaving the Emerald City, and I wasn't about to sit around waiting to hear how it turned out.

We crept through the forest as quietly as possible, and when we found the beast, it was as huge as the tiger claimed, and twice as ugly—legs like telephone poles, teeth a foot long, and all covered in coarse, black hair. If anything represented all my dark thoughts, or head wound or mental illness or *whatever*, it was this monstrosity.

And it was *asleep*.

The Lion put one claw up to his mouth in a silent *shush*, then quietly padded up to the spot where the beast's head was joined to its massive body with a neck as narrow as a wasp's waist. (I was fairly certain that whoever came up with this thing had never seen a close-up picture of actual spider anatomy, but that was neither here nor there.) He popped all five claws, raised his paw, and with one great blow cut the spider's head right off its body. The headless, elephantine spider thrashed about for a minute, then finally curled its legs up under its torso and lay still.

And that was it. We made our way back to the clearing where all the beasts of the forest were waiting for us to return. The Lion just gazed upon them regally and smiled.

"You're welcome," he said.

THE COUNTRY OF
THE QUADLINGS.

T he Lion promised to come back and rule over the animals as soon as I was safely on my way to Kansas. So now I had *two* kings slumming it with me (although I suppose the Scarecrow was technically a *mayor*). We passed through the forest safely, and when we stepped out of its gloom we found ourselves at the bottom of a steep, rocky hill.

"That will be a hard climb," the Scarecrow said. "But we must get over the hill, nevertheless."

So we started climbing. We had barely made it to the first rock, however, when a rough voice called out from behind it.

"Keep back!" A head peeked over the rock. "This hill belongs to us, and we don't allow anyone to cross it."

"Oh, we're crossing it," I said. I had been a bit out of sorts since watching the Lion kill the giant spider. Part of me suspected that the incident put a cap on the "Oz as a metaphor for my troubled mental state" portion of the journey, or possibly even disproved the entire theory of it. But I was tired of trying to figure out what all of this was supposed to be on an existential level. And at that point I had approximately zero patience for weird-looking dudes behind rocks telling me where I could and couldn't go.

"But you shall not!" the man insisted, stepping out from behind his outcropping. And "weird-looking" didn't even begin to describe him.

He was short and stout and had a big, flat head supported by a thick, wrinkly neck. He also had no arms at all. Was this a Quadling? No, I seemed to remember Beard Soldier saying something about odd people who prevented travelers from crossing their land. This guy seemed to fit the bill.

The Scarecrow, apparently, decided that he didn't look like much of a threat. "I'm sorry not to do as you wish," he said, "but we must pass over your hill whether you like it or not." He took one step forward, and as quick as lightning the man's head shot forward and his neck stretched out, hitting the Scarecrow like a battering ram and sending him tumbling back down the hill.

The Hammer Head guy just chuckled, and a chorus of boisterous laughter came from behind the other rocks. Hundreds of the armless little shits popped their heads up, all over the hillside.

The Lion roared and charged, but another head shot out, and he went rolling down the hill as if he'd been hit by a cannonball. The Tin Woodsman lifted his axe and tried to look threatening, but was hit in the gut by a head rocket before he could even take his first step, and went tumbling after.

Fuck *that*. I turned around and made my way slowly down the hill to join them.

We tried to find a pathway around the hill, but we were surrounded by rocks to the left and the right, and each one hid a sneering Hammer Head waiting to thwart our progress. There was no road open to us, except to the north, back into the forest.

"Perhaps it's time to call upon the Winged Monkeys," the Tin Woodsman suggested. "You have still the right to command them once more."

Ugh. Was this the challenge I had been saving my final monkey wish for the entire time? Or was this the challenge I needed my *second* monkey wish for, the one I'd wasted on balloon sewing, and I still had another impossible task left to undertake? To make it all worse, I was acutely aware that if I used the monkeys to get to Glinda now, I could have just as well called them back in the Emerald City and saved myself two days' worth of fucking hassle.

Of course, none of that was what I was *really* worried about. Would calling the monkeys mean I was *giving up*? Was it a signal to the book, or the coma, or the universe or whatever that I didn't have the strength left to go on, or the wits left to figure this out, so *fuck it, leave me stranded in Oz forever*?

I was starting to freak myself out again, so I took a deep breath and closed my eyes. *Forget about all the stupid theories. Forget about the book, the video game, the brainwashing, the coma, the madness. Forget it all. You've been transported to the magical land of Oz. You saw the Wizard, killed the Wicked Witch, missed your balloon ride, and Glinda is your last chance to get back home. Now you're stuck at the bottom of this hill. What do you do?*

You call the stupid Flying Monkeys.

I put on the cap, did the chant and the dance, and the sky immediately went dark with the silhouettes of winged primates. In a few moments the entire band stood before me.

"What are your commands?" inquired the King of the Monkeys, bowing low.

"You know," I said, "I had hoped to use my final wish to set you free."

"I knew as much the moment I looked into your eyes," he said. "All you must do to make it so is to command us never to obey the wearer of the Golden Cap again. Then we shall be free forever."

"Can I make, like, a deal with you? I set you free, and you promise to take me where I need to go, just as a favor?"

"It would behoove me to agree," the King said, "but Gayelette's spell forbade us to ever lie to the Cap's owner. Without the binding magic, the Winged Monkeys take orders from no one. We would just as soon leave you here to rot, and be on our way."

Nice. "Therefore, you must decide what you value more highly," he continued. "Our freedom, or your own desire."

I looked him straight in the eyes. "Carry me and my friends to Glinda the Good Witch."

You know what? Fuck that guy and his guilt trip. I had offered him what I thought was a square deal, but he decided he needed to be shitty about it. I wasn't the one who put the spell on them in the first place. And by my math, they had been commanded to do exactly *six things* in however many decades it had been since they were enchanted, and *four* of those were just in the last week. And they *weren't* particularly difficult.

The Winged Monkeys took the four of us, plus Toto, into their arms and flew us into the sky. It pissed off the Hammer Heads like crazy too—they yelled at us as we flew over, and shot their heads high into the air, hoping to knock us out of the monkeys' grasp. We flew over the hill, and into a country of lush fields, well-paved roads, and rippling brooks with strong, stone bridges across them. Everything was painted bright red, because *of course* they all color-coordinated. This *must* be land of the Quadlings.

They set us down at the gates of a big, handsome red castle. "This is the last time you can summon us," the Monkey King said. "So goodbye and good luck to you."

"Goodbye," I said. The monkeys rose into the air and flapped off toward the horizon. "And don't let the clouds hit you in the ass on the way out."

CHAPTER XXIII.

GLINDA THE GOOD WITCH GRANTS ARABELLA'S WISH.

he gates to Glinda's castle were guarded by three young women, dressed in sharp red uniforms trimmed with gold braids. The largest of the three approached us.

"Why have you come to the South Country?" she asked. She was polite, but something in her expression said that she was perfectly willing—and maybe just a little bit *eager*—to punch me in the face if I gave an answer she didn't like.

"We're here to see Glinda the Good Witch," I said. I had a full-grown lion and Conan the Fucking Axe Ninja at my side—I wasn't about to let this woman intimidate me.

She screwed up her face, like she was trying to decide if my response was punch-worthy. "Let me have your name, and I will ask Glinda if she will receive you," she said at last. She left through the gates, and the other two guards looked relieved. I had the distinct impression that we had just barely avoided fisticuffs.

After a few moments the guard returned to say that we were to be admitted at once. Along the way, she brought us to a changing room where we washed our faces and smoothed out our lumpy straw, and endeavored to make ourselves more or less presentable. The Woodsman oiled all his joints and pulled a bottle of tin polish from somewhere, buffing every inch of himself to a gleam. The Woodsman was *really* invested in making a good impression on Glinda the Good Witch.

When he finally finished, we followed the guard into a big room where Glinda was waiting for us on a throne of rubies.

Glinda was *crazy hot*, you guys. She wore a gauzy, white dress, and her red hair was done in flowing ringlets that cascaded over her soft, bare shoulders. She had deep blue eyes that I was already lost in, and *perfect fucking* skin. I wasn't gay or anything, but I was a *little bit* gay for Glinda the Good Witch.

The Tin Woodsman's hinged jaw literally dropped.

"What can I do for you, my child?" the Witch asked.

The prickly exterior I always worked so hard to maintain shattered under her gaze. "*I screwed it all up*," I said, trying to hold back the tears. "The stupid Wizard flew away without me, and we've just been wandering through forests and creepy doll countries—the Lion killed a giant spider, but even *that* was anticlimactic—and I don't know if I'm in a game or a coma or brainwashed or *crazy*, but this can't *possibly* be what happens in the book. And I'm tired, and filthy, and I stink, and used up all my monkey wishes, and *I don't want to be trapped here forever*." I fell to my knees, which was fine, because I guess I was pretty much begging at that point.

Glinda stepped off her throne, drew me close, and whispered into my ear. "Take heart, my sweet child. This is *exactly* what happens in the book."

And for some reason, *that* was what I needed to hear. Everything would be fine—*I was still just voyaging through literature*. The one theory I hadn't actually considered was that L. Frank Baum was just a shitty writer—he got to his big, dramatic conclusion but *hadn't met his word goal yet*, so he had

Dorothy wander the countryside for forty more pages, encountering all the half-baked shit that he hadn't managed to work into the plot.

It was a *revelation*. "So is that *it*?" I was almost afraid to ask. "Do I get to go *home*?"

Glinda gave me a little kiss on the forehead. "Bless your dear heart," she said. "I am sure I can tell you of a way to get back to Kansas. But, if I do, you must give me the Golden Cap."

"Certainly!" the Scarecrow exclaimed. "It is no use to us now, and when you have it you can command the Winged Monkeys three times!"

That's when it hit me. I could have just used up my three wishes, then *given the cap to the Scarecrow*, who could have used *his* three wishes and given the cap to the Tin Woodsman. I had been fretting over my precious monkey resources for days, but I could have had six additional wishes at least—*nine* if the Lion could manage to successfully navigate the hopping parts of the spell while balanced on his hind legs.

This is why I suck at computer games—Madeline would have made a much better Dorothy than I did. I handed the stupid hat to the Good Witch.

"I think I shall need their service just those three times," she said, smiling. "And you, gentle Scarecrow. What will you do when Dorothy has left us?"

"I will return to the Emerald City," he said. "For Oz has made me its ruler and the people like me. The only thing that worries me is how to cross the hill of the Hammer Heads."

"Then by means of the Golden Cap I shall command the Winged Monkeys to carry you to the gates of the Emerald City," Glinda said. "For it would be a shame to deprive the people of so wonderful a ruler."

The Scarecrow was absolutely giddy at the compliment. "Am I really wonderful?" he asked.

"You are... *unusual*," she replied. Oh my god, I *loved* Glinda the Good Witch. She turned to the Tin Woodsman. "And what will become of you when Dorothy leaves this country?"

Up to this point he had remained silent, apparently struck dumb by the Witch's beauty. Now he leaned on his axe for a moment, thinking. I was genuinely worried that he was going to hit on her.

Finally, he spoke. "The Winkies were very kind to me, and asked me to rule over them as their king when the Wicked Witch was no more. I am fond of the Winkies, and if I could get back again to the Country of the West, I should like nothing better than to rule over them forever."

"Wait," I said. "*What*? When did the Winkies *ask you to be their king*?"

"After they repaired me, just as I woke up," he said matter-of-factly. "They had never seen a man such as myself, and were quite taken aback in wonder."

So he had an offer of royalty *weeks ago*, and never even bothered to mention it, even as the others were being handed their own kingships left and right. The thought of it made me smile. The truth was, my Tin Man crush had mellowed a bit. I mean, I still thought he was hot like burning, and those hips would hold a special place in my sex dreams for years to come. But I had come to accept that in his eyes I'd always be a little girl—and not in the "he refuses to acknowledge the woman I've become" sense. When he looked at me he *literally saw a ten-year-old child*. No part of that scenario was a turn-on for me.

"Indeed, there has never *been* a man such as yourself," Glinda said. "My second command to the Winged Monkeys will be that they carry you safely to the land of the Winkies. Your brains may not be so large to look at as those of the Scarecrow, but you are really brighter than he is—when you are well-polished—and I am sure you will rule the Winkies wisely and well."

Then the Witch looked at the big, shaggy Lion and asked, "When Dorothy has returned to her own home, what will become of you?"

"Over the hill of the Hammer Heads," he said, "lies a grand old forest, and all the beasts that live there have made me their King. If I could only get back to this forest, I would pass my life very happily there."

"My third command to the Winged Monkeys," Glinda said, "shall be to carry you to your forest. Then, having used up the powers of the Golden Cap, I shall give it to the King of the Monkeys, that he and his band may thereafter be free forevermore."

Again, I felt like a dumbass. Evidently I had watched *Aladdin* too many times when I was a kid, because I had been all caught up in the whole idea of using my final wish to free the Genie. I could have just used my third monkey wish and then *given them the hat*, and it would have accomplished the same thing.

The Scarecrow and Woodsman and Lion all thanked Glinda earnestly for her generosity. "You are truly as kind as you are hot," I said. "But what about me? How do I get home?"

"Your silver shoes will carry you over the desert," Glinda replied. "If you had known their power you could have gone home the very first day you came to this country."

"I *did* know their power! I *tried* to use them the first day I came here!"

"But then I should not have had my wonderful brains!" the Scarecrow said. "I might have passed my whole life in the farmer's cornfield."

"And I should not have had my lovely heart," the Tin Woodsman added. "I might have stood and rusted in the forest 'til the end of the world."

"And I should have lived a coward forever," declared the Lion. "And no beast in all the forest would have had a good word to say to me."

"That's true," I said. "And I'm thrilled to death that I got to meet you all, and help you get your hearts' desire, plus a whole kingdom or whatever. But *for real*, I need to go home."

"The silver shoes have wonderful powers," the Good Witch said. "And one of the most curious things about them is that they can carry you to any place in the world in three steps, and each step will be made in the wink of an eye. All you have to do is to knock the heels together three times and command the shoes to carry you wherever you wish to go."

"So instead of passively stating how much I *like* Calabasas," I said, "I just needed to straight-up tell the shoes to *take me* there?" I was incredulous. "That's the *same thing*. That's the fucking *worst*."

Nevertheless, it was true. And now there was nothing left except the tearful goodbyes.

I took the Scarecrow's gloved hands in my own, foregoing the hug, since now in addition to his creepy face, he also had *pins and needles* poking out through his burlap head. "You've been a loyal companion and a kind, true friend," I said. "And there is *absolutely* no doubt in my mind that I will miss you least of all."

"That's fair," the Scarecrow said.

"I'm *kidding*," I said, giving him a careful hug in spite of it all. "I can't even count the times your cleverness saved us, and I'm glad you finally figured out how smart you are."

I turned and buried my head in the Lion's mane. "No one could ask for better protector, or a braver friend," I said. "Before the Klonopin, or after."

That just left the Tin Woodsman. And with all the tears flowing down his face, he was going to need about a gallon of oil. I threw my arms around him and hugged him tight. "Is there any chance you're patterned after some farmhand or something, out in the Midwest? With, I don't know, a *prosthetic hip replacement*?"

"Oh, Dorothy," the Woodsman said. "I didn't understand a *word* of that. How shall I ever get by without you?"

I disengaged from his embrace. "Well, you have a whole country to rule now, so... *representative democracy*? Seriously, all of you. Think about it."

I picked Toto up and tucked him under my arm. I was pretty sure he wasn't supposed to stay in Oz, and if I somehow ended up *owning a dog* after this was all over, I was okay with it. He was actually a pretty great little dog. Then I closed my eyes and clicked my heels together three times.

"*Take me home*," I said. Short, simple, and sweet.

Instantly I was whirling through the air, and all I could hear was the wind whistling past my ears.

HOME AGAIN.

The silver shoes took three wild, lurching steps through the void, then stopped so suddenly that I tumbled onto the grass and rolled over several times before I even figured out where I was.

Grass? There was no grass at *the mall.*

I opened my eyes to see a great, windswept plain under a vast, cloudless gray sky. There was a wooden farmhouse plopped down right in the middle of it that looked brand new and even a bit unfinished—which would make sense if the last one had recently been swept up in a tornado.

I was in fucking *Kansas.*

An old man was milking cows out in the barn, and Toto took off toward him, running. I didn't even remember what Dorothy's uncle's name was, but maybe Toto was technically *his* dog? A stout, silver-haired woman came out of the house with a watering pot, then dropped it when she saw me.

"My darling child!" she cried, tackling me in a running hug and covering my face with kisses. "Where in the world did you come from?"

It was kind of nice. "Uh, the Land of Oz, pretty much," I said. The moment stretched on. "But this is it, right? We're done? Roll credits?"

The credits did not roll. Something about all of it felt *very* wrong. "Well, don't just stand there," Auntie Em said. "Come inside and we'll draw you a nice, warm bath."

Oh, no. Oh, *fuck* no. If anything, the Depression-era Kansas dustbowl felt even more real than Oz had, and it was several times more depressing. I looked down at my feet—the silver shoes had *gone transparent*. They were fading away before my eyes. I clicked them together quickly times. "Take me to the mall in Calabasas! To *my* home!"

Nothing happened. Like the Flying Monkeys, *the shoes could only transport me to places inside the Oz Matrix*. There was no way I was going to let myself get trapped, and grow old and paranoid and bitter, like that fucking Wizard.

That fucking Wizard. Was *he* the key? Had he managed to escape, somehow, in his balloon? I clicked my heels again.

"Take me to the fucking Wizard!"

With another whoosh I was gone—I hoped this gust of wind wouldn't wreck Auntie Em's new house, but to be honest, I had my own shit to worry about. When I regained my senses this time, though, I didn't find myself safe on some patch of grass. I was high up in the sky, and somehow managed to just grab the edge of the balloon's passenger basket before falling toward my death on the inhospitable landscape far below.

"Dorothy! You found me!" Oz looked like hell. His hair was blowing wildly in the rough winds, his fine clothes were in tatters, and he stared at me like he was *fucking nuts*. The Wizard was *far* around the bend. It had been days since we'd left the Emerald City—had he been up in the balloon the entire time?

"I'm almost there!" he shouted. "See the hatch? That's where they send the weather from! But I'm going *through* it!"

I didn't see any hatch, but I did see the dark, inverted cone of a tornado—no, make that *three* tornadoes, whirling violently around us. The Wizard was somehow managing to pilot his craft between them.

My legs were still dangling off the edge of the basket. I tried to click my heels, but my socks just bumped together soundlessly. The silver shoes had either disappeared or fallen.

'They sent the weather to stop me!" Oz howled. "But not this time! *We won't be stopped!*"

One of the cyclones blew dangerously close, and the wind almost whipped me right off of my perch. Somewhere inside the maelstrom, I saw a flash of neon light. *EDUTAINMENT.*

"The tornadoes are the way out!" I cried, trying to be heard above the wind. "I'm sure of it! I saw the booth! From the mall!"

"I'm not going back to the mall!" he shouted. "They took me to Oz and just *left* me there, for *twenty-five years*, with nothing to do! And I want to know why!" He shook his fist at the sky. "You hear me? DO YOU HEAR ME? I want some goddamned answers!"

For the first time, I genuinely felt bad for him. The poor son of a bitch wasn't even the main character in *his own voyage through literature*. He pressed himself against the inside of the basket and reached toward me with one arm.

"Come *with* me, Dorothy! We'll figure out what this whole thing was, after all this time! *We'll find out together.*"

I *did* want to know what the hell was going on. And maybe there *was* a secret escape hatch somewhere up there in the sky. But I had stuff waiting for me at home. And given the choice between figuring out what the hell any of this was, and my life, I'd pick cell phones and Netflix and Tumblr, and Madeline, and my Mom.

Every time.

"I hope you find what you're looking for," I muttered under the wind. The tornado was almost upon me, and I flung myself away from the basket, falling backwards into the chaos of the cyclone's embrace, and immediately passing out.

* * *

At the end of the day, being shanghaied by a mall librarian and left for dead in a children's book was the worst thing that had ever happened to me. And, yeah, when I get the chance to look back at it with some perspective, I might decide it was the best thing that ever happened to me, too—meeting wonderful friends, growing as a person, all that bullshit. But whatever else it was, it was *definitely* the worst.

When I woke up, I was lying on a vast expanse of red sand. A green-skinned monster with tusks and a brass loincloth towered over me—he must have been fifteen feet tall, at least—and tapped my side with a long spear that he carried in two of his four arms.

So far, I amended. It was the worst thing that had ever happened to me *so far*.

ACKNOWLEDGEMENTS.

'd like to start by thanking Dawn Marie Pares and Melodie Ladner for their invaluable editorial assistance, and Mona Finden for bringing Arabella to life in her stunning cover art. Thanks also to Scott Gable for being a delightful convention companion and reliable surface off which to bounce things—his advice when I told him about this project was, "write it." And so I wrote it. And now it's writ.

Also, a special shout-out to Penni Harris Jones, who wrote a facebook post thanking the aforementioned Melodie for the "two tears in a bucket" line, which Penni had stolen for her own book. (Melodie confirmed that she got it from The Lady Chablis, and I went on to steal it from the whole lot of them. It's the circle of theft!)

Since my two-year-old child won't let me use a computer at home, huge swaths of this book were written in the cafes of Ballard, most notably Firehouse Coffee and Grumpy D's. Also the Ballard Public Library! I wrote a *ton* of this book at the Ballard Public Library. It's a really good public library.

Public libraries are the best.

AUTHORS.

M ATT YOUNGMARK is the creator of the Chooseomatic
Books series and the comic strip Conspiracy Friends. He lives
in Seattle, and intends to continue looting the corpses of long-
dead writers in his upcoming works. If you'd like to be alerted when his next
book comes out, please sign up for the mailing list at www.youngmark.com.

L. FRANK BAUM is the author of 55 books (including 14 set in the
land of Oz) and a number of stage plays. He was well-known in the early
20th century as a supporter of women's suffrage. Which sounds great, until
you run across the two editorials he wrote in 1890 for the *Aberdeen Saturday
Pioneer* in which he explicitly called for the genocide of Native Americans.

So, as Arabella would say, fuck that guy.

MORE FROM

MATT YOUNGMARK

CHOOSEOMATIC BOOKS
Zombocalypse Now
Thrusts of Justice
Time Travel Dinosaur

CONSPIRACY FRIENDS
Clandestine Maneuvers in the Dark
The Weird Turn Pro
Hot Vatican Nights

SHORTER THINGS
U, Robot
Tiny Quest

WWW.YOUNGMARK.COM

62787138R00094

Made in the USA
Lexington, KY
17 April 2017